CRY TO THE NIGHT WIND

T.H. SMITH

VIKING KESTREL

VIKING KESTREL

Penguin Books Canada Limited, 2801 John Street,
Markham, Ontario Canada L3R 1B4

Penguin Books, Harmondsworth, Middlesex,
England

Viking Penguin Inc., 40 West 23rd Street,
New York, New York 10010 U.S.A.

Penguin Books Australia Ltd., Ringwood, Victoria,
Australia

Penguin Books (N.Z.) Ltd., Private Bag, Takapuna,
Auckland 9, New Zealand

First published by
Penguin Books Canada Limited, 1986

Copyright ©Thomas H. Smith, C.M., 1986

Printed and bound in the United States of America

Canadian Cataloguing in Publication Data

Smith, Thomas H.
  Cry to the night wind

ISBN 0-670-80750-8

I. Title.

PS8587.M585C79   1986   jC813'.54   C85-090789-6
PZ7.S655Cr   1986

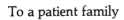

To a patient family

CRY TO THE NIGHT WIND

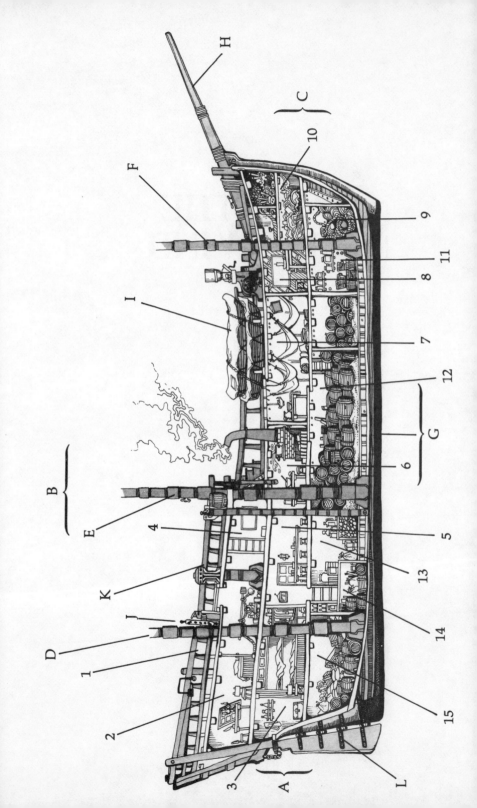

H.M.S. *LANGLEY*

1. Helm
2. Captain's quarters
3. Officers' quarters
4. Companionway (passage)
5. Officers' mess (dining)
6. Ship's galley (kitchen)
7. Fo'c's'le (crew's quarters)
8. Bosun's quarters
9. Anchor line storage
10. Sail repair storage
11. Polish and cleaning storage
12. Bully beef and food lockers
13. Officers' mess pantry
14. Valuables locker
15. Officers' "extra" food allowance
A Stern or Aft
B Midships
C Bow
D Mizen (aft) mast
E Mainmast
F Foremast
G Keel
H Bowsprit
I Cutters (longboats)
J Ship's wheel
K Capstan (winch)
L Rudder

One

H.M.S. *Langley* sailed proudly over the wild sea, leaning hard to the wind. Her bow rose up into the air and plunged downward, flinging salt spray over an aged sailor as he watched for jagged rocks. David, a young boy of eleven, clung to the rail behind him, his blond hair swept back by the breeze.

"That last one was a big wave, Grimsbey!" the boy laughed. "My shirt is soaked."

"Aye, lad. The swells build up as they near the coastline. Once that fog lifts, you will see a strange land, you will."

"Father says there are Indians living on shore. He says they are very friendly!"

"Maybe, m'lad, but I be not so sure of that as your father now," Grimsbey said as he turned around. "A mate of mine who sailed with Captain Cook himself tells it a little different, he does. Aye... three Jacks, all good men, disappeared into thin air one morning, they did. Poor blighters. Not a sign left of them. Not a hair of their heads! Hang on, m'lad."

A tremendous wave pounded against the heavy timber, then fell back.

"Did the Indians attack the ship?" the boy asked.

"Nay, not that time. The lads grew restless and took themselves a small cutter and rowed ashore. Not even the boat was found. Nothing!"

"We will be all right, won't we?"

"If we keep our eyes open and stay with the ship, we should do right well. Now don't worry your head."

David tugged at his damp shirt as he wandered back towards the stern. He was a sturdy boy for his age, with broad shoulders, a solid frame and a determined air about him. His mop of golden hair blew over a ruddy face which boasted a broad smile and large, bold eyes as blue as the summer sea.

Without warning, the cover of grey cloud scattered and a burst of sunlight beamed down upon the ship, turning its dull canvas sails into a mass of brilliant white. Gulls swooped down out of nowhere and dodged in and out of the rigging.

"Take in the mainsails! Lift your feet, lads! Look alive!"

Two dozen British tars scrambled up into the web of rope ladders and sidestepped along flimsy line strung below the yards. Knives flashed and necklaces clinked as they furled the heavy canvas. David gazed up at them, marvelling anew at their courage as they clung for dear life, dangling out over the sea as the *Langley* heeled, then perching above the deck once more as she righted herself.

"Want to climb aloft to the mainyard, Davie?"

The young sailor turned to see his father leaning on the helm. "Pardon? Oh, Father! . . . I don't think so right now, sir," and, changing the subject, "Are we almost there?"

"Almost indeed," Captain Spencer replied. "Look to your starboard — that point of land. We go about those rocks and behind them we shall find a narrow entrance to a sheltered inlet. No more riding the waves for a while."

"Oh, I'm getting used to it, Father. I haven't been seasick for a fortnight, have I?"

"Right you are, Davie. Ah, even captains suffer the willies, you know. A friend of mine stows himself below two days out from land on every voyage. Wait...Mr Perkins, see to that capstan forward!"

"Aye aye, Captain."

David's father moved to the stern rail high above the swirling water to check for signs of seaweed trailing off the rudder. The boy followed him and rested against the rail for a few moments, deep in thought. Then he pulled gently on his father's sleeve.

"Grimsbey says there are dangerous natives living in those inlets. He says a person can disappear forever here!"

The captain continued his inspection as he spoke. "Grimsbey is a great storyteller. I sailed these very waters under Captain Vancouver not more than four years ago — the voyage of 1793. The natives welcomed us and traded gifts with the ship's company." He straightened up and grinned at David. "A good lot they were indeed."

"But did you sail up that inlet over there?" the boy insisted, pointing to the channel ahead.

"Well, not beyond the entrance, but they're all alike — quiet as tombs. Now, keep clear of the lines, Davie. I have to attend to the ship. Away with you to your duties. See to your chores below."

"But I've finished, sir."

"Very well then. But keep clear until we have secured the sheets."

Captain Spencer strode down the rolling deck, leaving David to his own thoughts. England was now a bare memory

after six long months at sea. He remembered the weeks before
the departure, the noisy arguments between his mother and
father about whether David should go along on this last survey of the mysterious northwest coast of North America. His
mother had pleaded with his father to leave him at home for
just one more year, but Captain Spencer had made up his
mind. He himself had sailed with the Navy at twelve years of
age, and David would be twelve after ten months out.

Next to his mother, David missed his small spaniel most.
The pup was a friendly ball of fur, and the two of them had
spent night and day together, running through the tall grasses
of the English fields and down the narrow lanes that wound
past the old stone houses. David had planned to bring the dog
with him, but he had soon learned that there would be no
dog aboard the *Langley*. It would bother the cats, those wild,
vicious villains, tolerated because they kept the rats and other
vermin in check.

Then there were the Beecham boys, Philip, Harold and Ber-
ty, who lived in the great manor down the lane. He would miss
them too. Their father was also a captain, though his ship was
a great flag of the fleet and carried three tiers of cannon. . .

"Danger hoooo!" a voice rang out. "Look to your starboard!"

David thought about the good life he had left behind, imagined the smell of his mother's cooking, wondered if his father
would ever understand him, how he felt, how lonely he was.
He didn't really know his father, having seen him only five or
six times in as many years. Some of the captain's voyages
lasted twenty or thirty months and, when he did return, the
boy sometimes had trouble getting used to him. Now here he
was, quartered with a man who was almost a stranger to him.
It was not always a comfortable feeling.

"Look to your portside, hoooo!"

The boy glanced up and quickly ran to the port rail.

Two

*I*t seemed like forever since the *Langley* had bade farewell to the shores of England. First she had run down the coast of Spain without so much as a rainy day, heading bravely into the Atlantic for her long crossing to South America. David was kept busy attending to the officers' table and cleaning up the master's quarters, a large aft cabin he shared with his father. In addition, he was called upon once each day to scrub down the galley, a duty put into practice by Captain Cook.

There were two other boys on board, but they were "London rats," young orphans who had been living in empty barrels strung along cobblestone lanes. They were treated like common thieves, and Captain Spencer threatened them with great "divilment" if they so much as spoke a word to his son. That suited them, for they did not want anyone to think that they would be seen with such as the son of a sea captain.

The boredom of the routine on board had been broken one afternoon when a lone ship appeared off the *Langley*'s starboard quarter. She flew no flag at her stern and gave no signal, just followed the British vessel hour after hour, causing Captain Spencer to break out the guns and post all hands to the rails to keep an eye on her. The captain figured that if she were a pirate ship, she would know that the *Langley* would not be carrying gold bullion while she was heading westward. Only vessels returning east to Europe transported the rich treasures that hungry marauders sought so eagerly. Sure enough, the unwelcome company steered away before dusk and disappeared into the night.

All hands drew a long breath when the watch was put down, for the *Langley* was not equipped to fend off a pirateer. David, however, was of two minds. He was pleased that he would not find himself being fed to the sharks, but on the other hand he did want to have a closer look at a famous brigand. He smiled to himself as he dreamed about telling the Beecham boys how, single-handed, he had fought off a horde of bloodthirsty buccaneers!

Another stroke of luck befell David when the ship rounded Cape Horn off the tip of South America. For weeks he had been listening to stories about how the merging of two great oceans at the Horn churned up tremendous seas that could toss a vessel against the rocks like flotsam in the wind. Seldom were there calm days in this region, but the *Langley* was awarded a rippled sea and light but adequate wind, and she passed through the channel without a hitch.

David was beginning to wonder if the oceans ever acted up at all when, to his initial delight, the Pacific began to conjure up a series of high seas, picking the heavy ship up and sliding her down into deep troughs, leaving the lad's stomach somewhere between the two. For weeks the *Langley* fought the fierce gales from the north, crashing headlong into murky, salty blackness, her crew facing the wind and spray with clenched teeth. After a good tumble down the main deck one afternoon,

David fast became one of the volunteers who wore safety belts and harnesses, for once across the hard teak into the scuppers was enough punishment for a lifetime.

The high seas had subsided and a warm sun was beaming down on the ship as it neared the Sandwich Islands in the mid-Pacific. Much to the disappointment of everyone aboard, Captain Spencer elected to keep well clear of the inviting shores, remembering the sad fate of Captain Cook not too many months before. David had to be satisfied with a mere glimpse of the colourfully garbed natives as they ventured out in their massive outriggers. A single shot from the *Langley's* cannon warned them to advance no further, and the younger islanders who were swimming beside the twin hulls scrambled aboard just in time to be rushed ashore.

After a short rest in the lee of a small outer island, the sailing ship weighed anchor and was soon dipping and rolling to the northeast towards the mysterious coastline of America. The sea was fairly calm for the time of year and the winds brisk, making the voyage an uneventful one for the time being. Perhaps that was a good thing, considering what was in store for the young sailor. Now here they were, about to enter an unexplored inlet, not knowing what to expect...

The *Langley* slowed to a turtle's pace as she picked her way among the black rocks, her lookout hanging from his lofty perch, warning, "Danger ho! Look to your starboard! Come alive!"

A dozen men bent over the rails as the barnacled hull scraped past a stump adrift off the bow. Captain Spencer stood fast by the wheel, silent, his eyes fixed on the narrow opening in the cliffs.

"Not much room to move, Captain Spencer, sir," the mate said quietly.

"Enough, Mr Perkins."

"Aye aye, sir."

First Officer Perkins reddened and looked away, hairs bristling under his collar. Perhaps he was annoyed with himself for forgetting that he was serving under a tough seaman who did not welcome advice from anyone aboard his ship. Unlike Captain Vancouver, Spencer was a fellow who avoided small talk and never argued a point with anyone. His word was final.

The vessel's stern was picked up by a mountainous swell and the small ship almost flew into the channel with the force of it. She settled on calm water in a new world, a peaceful place bordered on all sides by rock cliffs over a hundred feet high, topped by towering firs. A lone eagle soared on the breeze, squawking a protest at the intruders. Salmon jumped up into the air and splashed noisily into the silver water, leaving a series of rings behind them. A cormorant flew across the inlet, settling on a bobbing log off the far shore.

"Grimsbey, how far does this channel go through the mountains?" the boy asked the old bosun as he approached the helm.

"Huh? How far? Maybe a mile, maybe a hundred, m'lad. That's what we've come to seek out. Strange place, this. Chills me bones!"

"Why do you say that?"

"I just feel it. This here's not a good spot for a ship the likes of ours now. No breeze to move us. No means to turn about save the long boats towing our bow. We're helpless, we are."

David glanced about, first at the clifftops, then back at the slim gap between the rock walls that led to the ocean. "But we have to chart the inlet so that other ships can come here. That's what Father says!"

"Aye, and who will ever want to come in here, I ask you?" Grimsbey scowled. "Even Captain Cook himself said there was nothing worth the journey to this black coast. We should leave it all to the Spaniards!"

"Grimsbey!" a voice rang out.

"Aye aye, sir!"

"Prepare the cutter. We'll lower away with five men to sound the bottom for a safe anchorage," the captain ordered.

"Aye aye, sir!"

"Davie, you may join the cutter if you wish."

"Thank you, Father!" the boy grinned. He ran after the old sailor and helped pull the canvas off the longboat, working alongside the crew. Soon the slim craft was free and launched on the smooth surface. When all seven souls were aboard, she was pushed away from the *Langley* and oars lowered to the water. One man let out a loud cry and grinned as his voice bounced back off the rock wall in a shimmering echo. Grimsbey growled at him and the fellow set to with his oar.

"We'll ride a wide circle about the ship, boys. Lean a little on the starboard oars," Grimsbey said firmly. "Walters, put your back into it."

"As you say, old man," the sailor muttered.

Grimsbey eyed him and looked away. "David, m'lad, take up that lead and heave her over the side."

The boy picked up the five-pound slug and dropped it over the gunnel, watching the heavy line slip through his fingers. Suddenly the cord fell slack. "She's hit bottom!"

"Let's see — two...four...almost six fathoms at low tide."

David retrieved the line and let it drop again, calling the depth over and over until the bosun had a picture of the bottom in his mind's eye. The *Langley* would not run afoul at the ebb tide's low, he decided, and he ordered the cutter back to the ship. "Walters, pick up that oar and work it. Take your share of the load!"

"You going to make me, old man?" the seaman sneered.

"You defy me, sailor?"

"You would fight the likes of me, you old fool?"

The bosun rose slowly to his feet and glared down at the brazen sailor. Walters gazed up at the crimson face and his temper quickly cooled. The old man stood five foot ten, a giant for the time, and weighed close to two hundred pounds. His arms were the size of barrels. His grey hair had thinned somewhat, but he made up for it by sporting a fine full beard that jutted out to challenge any man alive. His eyes twinkled and his bulbous nose twitched as he sniffed the wind for coming storms. And, as rough as the old barnacle appeared on the outside, within was stored a warm heart and good thought, virtues David had come to appreciate in the sometimes lonely life he led on board.

Walters was readying another volley when a thin wisp of a man piped up from behind him. "Back off, mate. Know when you've said enough."

Walters spat on the floor boards and dropped the blade of his oar into the water. He looked away as Grimsbey was about to speak. The bosun decided to save his breath instead.

Once the clinker boat had come alongside the *Langley*, a line was heaved up to the deck and, one by one, all hands climbed the swinging ladder. Finally Grimsbey pulled his massive bulk up to the toprail.

"Captain, sir, we have five to eight fathoms all 'round. She should ride right fine as she be, sir."

"Excellent, Grimsbey. Well done. The men can stand to for their rum ration. Sound the assembly!"

"Aye aye, sir. Sound your pipe, sailor."

The squeal of the whistle flew out over the narrow waterway and resounded back to the vessel, bringing forty hands to the heel of the mainmast. Quickly, a wooden barrel was carried out and laid at the feet of the captain. Grimsbey knelt and took the ladle.

"Swift. . . Bixby. . . Link. . . Peters. . ." On the list went, each man stepping forward with his small pewter cup held out for a tot of the thick, syrupy rum. Then the call ceased.

"You forgot me, bosun," a voice complained.

"Who you be, man?" Grimsbey said without looking up.

"Walters!"

"I didn't forget you, Walters. I overlooked you. That be a little different."

Captain Spencer glanced down. "Trouble, Grimsbey?"

"Nothing now, sir. It's all shipshape."

The captain turned to Walters just as the angry crewman spun about and walked away. Suddenly the bitter sailor whirled around, drew his knife and sent it shimmering across the deck, narrowly missing Grimsbey's head. It struck the mainmast and held fast, quivering to a standstill.

"That will do, Walters!" Captain Spencer roared. "You men there — take him and cast him into the brig at once. I'll have none of that aboard my ship!"

Walters offered no resistance as he was tackled by three of his shipmates and trundled off below to a small wooden cage near the keel. David felt his heart pound within his chest, the thud of the knife still ringing in his ears.

"Well, Davie," said his father, taking him by the shoulder, "you can sound the bottom with the lead and chain. Grimsbey tells me you did a fine job. We'll make a seaman out of you yet."

Late that night, David lay awake on his bunk, his eyes blinking in the darkness. He did not hear the mournful call of the loon or the playful splashing of the sea otters across the water.

His head was spinning with pictures of mutineers and pirates, glittering swords crashing down on helpless victims, the vision made all the more frightening as he recalled the grizzly, scarred face of Walters. Like many of the crew, he had been rooted out from the underground cells of London's prisons and pressed into service in the King's Royal Navy. Some of them were thieves and murderers, and a few months at sea did nothing to change their hearts.

The boy wondered how his father would continue to manage to keep such a crowd in line for another twelve months, for that was how long the voyage would last. He recalled the talk about the *Bounty* and how his father's friend, Captain Bligh, was cast out in a longboat with a few loyal men and forced to find his way five thousand miles back to safety. Then there were the terrifying tales of pirates and the plank . . .

Would his father be able to keep the *Langley* under command? David closed his eyes, giving in to sleep. The morning would soon bring an answer to his question.

Three

CCCCRRRAAACCCCKKKK!

The whip drew back and curled as it was flung once more towards Walters. His sentence was a flogging with the cat-o'-nine-tails, nine leathery thongs tied to a short handle.

CCCRRRAAACCCKKK!

The man made no noise, his arms strung up to the mast, his bare back creased with swelling red welts. He jerked each time the whip connected with his skin and every man winced, feeling the sting deep in his bones. Not many of them had escaped the feel of the lash, however long they had been at sea. They stood now, shaking with fear, counting silently as the whip found its mark. Twenty-one . . . twenty-two . . . twenty-three. . . . They eyed the captain as he stood stiffly at attention, his eyes focused on the culprit, his jaw firm. Each man listened for the words that would call a halt to it.

"That will do, Wiggins. Release him," Captain Spencer said calmly. "All right, men. To your duties."

The crewmen were now more than eager to get back to

their chores of mending canvas, splicing lines and caulking
the seams in the hull. Walters was assisted to the brig by two
men, his feet half dragging along the deck as he moved. David
watched him until he disappeared. The boy had been told to
remain in his father's cabin aft, but curiosity had won out
and he had crouched hidden behind a capstan throughout the
ordeal. Finally, when the way was clear, he raised himself off
his trembling knees and crept down the gangway. Suddenly,
he came face to face with Grimsbey.

"Ooops! Sorry, Grimsbey. I didn't see you."

"No harm done, m'lad. 'Twas a rough thing for you to
behold up there," the old man nodded.

"Me? Oh, I didn't — I mean, I wasn't really..."

"You've been kneeling by the capstan all the while. You have
grease on your trousers. Look at 'em. Truth now."

David reddened. "Well, ah...I guess so, Grimsbey."

"Best you get to your quarters and change those togs afore
your father waylays you. I'll scrub 'em down with me own
gear if you'll save 'em for me."

"Yes. Thank you, Grimsbey. I, well..."

"Speak out, m'lad."

Tears welled up in David's eyes and he looked away in
shame.

"What be bothering you?" Grimsbey asked gently.

"Why? Why did he do that? Why did my father order the
whipping? He...he could have kept him in the brig, couldn't
he? How could he be so cruel?"

The wise old bosun rubbed his grey beard with a gnarled
hand and shook his head. "No, no," he said quietly. "He be not
cruel. Far from it. Why, your father had every right to hang
that fellow up on the yardarm for what he done, aye. Walters
there could right be a dead man and no one here would have
raised an eyebrow! No, laddie, your father, he took it light on

him for all of that. Let 'em off too easy, lad, and they'll take your ship and your life if they feel the need. You must believe it. Hark now . . ."

The old sailor glanced behind him to see a pair of black boots descending the stairs. "Away with you, my boy," he whispered and, turning quickly, "Excuse me, Captain, I was wondering when we be getting under way with the survey this morning? I have a list here of the crews for the longboats. The craft be stocked and ready, sir."

"Good fellow! We can embark at four bells. Let us see who you have lined up here," Captain Spencer replied, totally unaware of the boy clambering out of his greasy trousers behind the cabin door.

Grimsbey held out his fingers and, one at a time, he slowly ticked off a number of worthies. ". . . and there be Peters, he's a good man for cutting the bush there, and then we have Morgan. Now there's a worker . . . ah, me thinks Ford and his friend, Bixby . . ."

"Yes, yes!" the captain prompted impatiently.

"And Longberry . . . Shaft . . . that should do it!"

"Fine, fine, Grimsbey."

The bosun guessed that David had had enough time to change his soiled clothes, so he moved aside, allowing the captain to squeeze by him in the narrow passageway. Captain Spencer pushed the oak door wide and stepped into the cabin to find David seated comfortably on the cushioned bench at the leaded window. The boy spoke without turning about.

"Father, may I go out on the survey today with Grimsbey?"

"Nay, Davie. You must stay with the ship. You may keep watch with Mr Perkins this time out. Best until we know the lay of the land, my boy."

"Yes, sir," David said glumly. "Perhaps I might go out tomorrow."

"We'll see. Now off with you," Spencer frowned as he tousled the boy's hair.

David rose from the ledge and, with head bowed, he shuffled across the teak floor and left the cabin. The companionway was dimly lit, dark enough to hide someone alone with his thoughts. He sank down on a hard bench below the hatch opening and leaned his head back on the wall behind him. His tongue ran over his upper lip as he tried to figure out what his father expected of him. At one moment, he was to act like a man, lending a hand with the chores, dragging heavy barrels of salted grub to the galley, pushing grimy mops across the rolling cabin decks. At the next, he was to "act his age," too young to go out on the surveys along the coastline, too little to stay up to watch the sailors' hornpipe and listen to their chanteys and their stories. What was he supposed to do? And then there was the whipping of Walters. Grimsbey was probably right about it, but David still didn't like seeing his father use such harsh measures. He clenched his fists and banged them against the wall behind him, shutting his eyes in frustration. Then the sunlight streaming down through the open hatch caught his attention, and he relaxed a bit. Surely things would sort themselves out.

David climbed the steps of the gangway and found himself on the cool deck. The wind had risen and the white ensign was flapping noisily. Skinny Havlock was polishing the helm, each prong of the wheel glistening under a thick coat of oil. Three men sat on their haunches, tugging at strands of yellow hemp while another chipped away at a barrel of bully beef.

The lonely young boy moved idly to the rail and peered down into the green-black water. Suddenly a small creature popped its nose through the surface and ogled him through round glassy eyes. David watched as it tossed its head and rolled onto its back. A baby seal! Then, with a quick flip of its tail, it was under again and before the boy could count to five, the little animal reappeared a few yards off, slapping a fin against its side.

"Perhaps he's hungry," David thought to himself. "I should find something for him to eat."

Three quick jumps and a slide down a railing brought him to the galley entrance. He remembered the fresh fish the cook had caught earlier in the morning and followed his nose to a low wooden crate. A fat grilse was yanked from the sticky lot and the kitchen thief quickly padded up the steps and across the deck to the rail.

The plump round head with the saucery eyes was circling around, the pup somehow sensing that its new friend would return. "Come over here. Come on!" the boy greeted it.

David swung the shiny wet grilse over the side and threw it into the water inches away from the pup's rubbery black nose. In seconds, the hungry animal had snapped up the morsel of fish and wolfed it down. Next followed a performance of wild antics, rolls, turns and dives that would do justice to a travelling circus. David laughed as he followed the agile little creature until he could see the silvery head no longer. Then his attention turned to other things, to thoughts about the cutters out on the inlet, Walters down in the brig, Indians. . .

Four

"More fish! I'll be turning into a blooming fish meself if this keeps up, mate," a young sailor complained.

"This one here's a salmon," Grimsbey announced. "Weighed him in at five stone. Four foot long from tip to tail, he was — as big as Davie Spencer!"

Suddenly the fo'c's'le fell hushed. All eyes turned to the bottom of the ladder where Walters stood, shirt in hand, face drawn in a long scowl, shoulders drooping. He glanced about, then shuffled to his place at the long table. Once seated, his back became too visible, an ugly reminder to all sitting about. The dim lamplight cast strange shadows over the torn flesh, some of it dangling down in red strings. No one wished to open a conversation. No one dared. The newcomer reached out, took a crust of dry bread and began to chew slowly.

One by one the men rose and found an excuse to go topside until only three were left — Walters, bony Havlock and "one-eyed" Sam Link, a former pirate who had roamed the Caribbean as a teenager. Link climbed to his feet, moved over to the hatch and glanced up. He returned to the table and slumped down on a narrow bench opposite Walters.

"Cook or Vancouver, they would have done different, they would," Link began. "You'd get no cat-o'-nine-tails for what you done."

Walters stared vacantly ahead.

"If I were you," Link continued, "I'd wait me chance and do old Grimsbey in, aye." He scraped under a fingernail with his bone-handled knife.

"No use trying the likes of that, Link," Havlock broke in. "The whole ship'd know who done it!"

"Well, Walters don't have to do the deed himself," Link argued. "I just says it should be done, that's all."

Walters stirred, eyed Link for a brief second and then walked to his bunk. He flopped down on his stomach and shut his eyes.

Late afternoon was no cooler than midday had been, and David kept his lonely watch from the shelter of a fold of mended canvas, his clothes fairly glued to his skin with moisture. He did not recognize the noise at first, but when he listened more closely, he likened it to an impatient dog wanting into the house. Soon a pair of trousered legs was dangling over the rail of the deck, bare feet gripping the netting, allowing arms free to toss chunks of fresh fish into the water below. Each time a bit struck the surface, a round, silver-grey head popped up and sniffed the plump morsel, snapped it up and was gone.

"Come on! Here, little seal!" David called.

Now the boy eased himself back along the bowsprit until he could poise safely, directly above the animal. Next he ran aft, ninety feet or more, and leaned over again. "Come on, seal, here's your dinner! I'm up here!" Then David's eyes widened and his ears tingled when the grateful pup returned his call with a barking of its own. Instantly another slice of meaty salmon was thrown down.

"Don't drop any of that fish onto the deck, Davie!" Captain Spencer smiled.

"Oh, hello, sir! I didn't see the boats coming in. Father, over here...Look what I've found!" David grinned as he moved farther along the rail. "He's a beauty, right?"

"What's this? A seal. Indeed!"

"Watch this. Wait!" David said as he held a shiny grilse out over the railing. "He can roll over. Come on...do it! There. What do you think of that?"

"He's a fine performer, lad," Captain Spencer admitted dryly.

"May I bring him up here on the deck?" the boy asked, half of his body hanging precariously over the side.

"What would you do with a wet seal on these hot boards, I ask you? He would burn his flippers within minutes. No, no, he would not be content up here at all, I'm afraid. He belongs over there on those rocks. His family is probably keeping a weather eye on him this very minute. Now scrub up and tend to your lessons for an hour."

"But Father, it's summer!" David protested. "All my friends in England are out of school."

"Ah, but you have already enjoyed six months' holiday from school, Davie. Now another two minutes here, and then stow yourself below and do your duty." Given the tone of his father's voice, David knew this would be the last word on the matter.

But for now, he was both amazed and pleased with himself as he watched the small animal waiting for his next move. It reminded him of his pup far away, so ready to play, so eager to eat. At last he had a friend who understood him, and a strange one at that, for David had never more than glimpsed seals in the distance off the shores of Scotland. And now here he was, taming one of them to answer at a mere word.

Perhaps another quarter of an hour slipped by the busy pair, one high on the wooden deck and the other splashing about in the warm water of the inlet. So intent was the young sailor that he forgot his father's directions completely, remembering only when the familiar voice called an order to some wayward seaman in the bows. The sound was enough to send him flying down the companionway and into the sunlit cabin.

"Arithmetic!" he muttered to himself. "In the middle of summer too."

"Arf, arf, arf!"

The boy jumped up to the window in time to see the seal pup almost dancing on the surface of the water, tossing its head back and forth. David knocked on the window and waved to it. Then he dashed back to the table and furiously scribbled his sums, filling page after page. His quilled pen dipped into the bottle and scratched over the paper so quickly that he finished his assignment in record time and was on his way back to the deck. Bright strips of sunlight filtered through the trees to warm the air, but the planks of the deck were cool and it was easy for bare feet to run from rail to rail. David hoisted himself up so that his toes could dangle free in the light breeze. A white gull spread its wings and swooped down, hoping for a share of the fish dinner, but the little seal was nowhere to be seen.

David hopped, skipped and jumped to the opposite rail and peered down. "Here, seal!" he cried. "Here I am!"

Suddenly the surface of the water broke and a shiny head bobbed up into the daylight. A brilliant idea struck the boy. Why not climb down the ladder . . .

With one quick glance up and down the deck, David slipped over the heavy supports until his toes found the first damp step of the flimsy ladder. Down he climbed until one foot touched the water, and instantly the small seal swam over to nudge his heel. The water was so warm, the boy thought, almost like a tub bath. This was more than he could bear. He worked his way back up the ladder to the deck and took another quick look around. Finding no one nearby, he unbuttoned his shirt and stepped out of his heavy trousers. All the wild stories about killer whales and devil fish were forgotten as the white leggings flew down over the side. One short jump and David was in the water.

He bubbled to the surface of the placid inlet and treaded water, grateful that he had learned to swim down at the old wharf by his village. Now he and the seal pup dove, rolled about, ducked and splashed and then floated on their backs, studying each other, their stomachs catching the last rays of sunlight. They submerged again, leaving a trail of small bubbles, and somersaulted over and over before coming up for another breath of air. Down they dove again, arms and flippers tucked in at their sides, bodies arched to turn a full circle beneath the calm surface. They surged through schools of small fish, sending them in a hundred different directions. The boy waved an arm into the air and then drifted under, pretending to drown, and the little animal quickly swam beneath him, frantically nudging him back up towards the fresh air.

Finally, David, the weaker of the two swimmers, grew tired and, after a playful push, he swam for the ladder on the opposite side of the ship. He held his head high so that he would not pass the rope steps but when he came to the spot where he remembered the ladder to be, there was nothing to climb up. The steps were gone! At first David thought he might be mistaken. Perhaps the ship had swung around with the tide. He retraced his path back to the starboard side, the seal pup following at his heels, only to find that there was no ladder in sight. Soon he felt his legs beginning to tire, and treading water became hard work.

David hovered at the spot for another minute or two, wondering what he should do. Because he did not have permission to be in the water, he dared not call out, yet he knew he could not tread water much longer. Suddenly, the seal pup nuzzled him in the side of his ribs and then darted ahead to circle under the anchor chain, returning to nudge the boy on. David began to follow the pup and once again it pivoted below the anchor.

"That's it!" the boy thought as he reached out to pat the pup. Then, with one foot solidly tucked into an iron link of the chain, he drew himself up until he was able to swing a leg over the bowsprit netting. He hung down by his knees, waved to his friend and leaped to the deck in a single step. There, not more than ten yards to the stern, stood Walters, the rope ladder curled up at his feet. The man half-heartedly pushed a mop across the boards, sneering at the boy as he laboured, a toothpick hanging down from his lower lip. He finally moved off, leaving David to gather up his clothes. The exhausted swimmer stooped down and then stepped back in shock. His best pants and shirt were sopping with rancid vinegar. As he poked at the soggy remains, he discovered that his white shirt was also smeared with thick black grease from the capstan.

In his panic, David began to wring out the heavy garments. This seemed to do nothing for their appearance, so he spread them out along the wide railing, pressing the smelly juice out of them with his hands. Again his efforts proved useless, the pressure merely serving to spread the black grease into his skin, further damaging the soiled pants, which up to now had absorbed only the fuming vinegar. As he fumbled with the mess, he found himself beginning to tremble from head to toe. His body grew suddenly cold as he finally recognized how close he had come to a frightening end. Walters could have been watching all along as he struggled in the water, knowing full well that he was in serious trouble.

For a moment he thought he should report the incident to his father in spite of the scolding he was bound to receive, but then he remembered the strict rule of his stern mentor: "Never tell tales on people." David chose to remain silent. Perhaps later, he thought, he might share his worries with Grimsbey. With a heavy sigh, he swept the ruined clothes into his arms and bolted for the cabin. He burst through the doorway almost into the lap of his father, who was sitting at his desk.

"Swimming, my boy?"

David eyed the floor. "Yes, sir." He remembered the clothes tucked under his arm and tried to ease them behind his back.

"I don't recall giving you permission."

"No, sir," he answered, avoiding a cold stare.

"There are rules, Davie, and they must be obeyed. They are laid on for your protection. The next episode of this kind will bring you stiff punishment. Do you understand?"

"Yes, sir."

"Very well." Captain Spencer turned to his charts. "By the way, lad, it would be best not to coax your young seal to loll around the anchorage. He must not be seen to swim about too much or he'll anger the cook. Seals chase away the fish, you know."

"But Father, he's too young to cause any harm. He's only two feet long himself!" David exclaimed.

"Well, keep him clear of the fishing lines or the cook will serve him for dinner. Now, off with those wet togs and into your bunk."

David carefully edged his way to his bed, continuing to

conceal the soiled garments behind his back. He eased them to the floor and pushed them beneath the bunk with his foot. Once he had climbed into his nightclothes, he stuffed the gummy shirt and pants into a bag, hid them below and slid beneath the covers.

"Hmmmmm. . . what's that odour, Davie? Have you been lying about the deck? I can smell the stuff as if it was in this very room. Vinegar."

"Vinegar, sir?"

"Yes. The men are soaking the boards with vinegar to keep down infection. Well?"

"I. . . I left my pants and shirt on the deck when I went swimming," the boy answered fearfully.

"Let's see here. . ." His father rooted out the canvas bag and withdrew the offending clothing. "My word! What have you done? These are your best togs. Your mother worked for weeks to ready them for the voyage! Shame, my son. And look at the grease on this shirt."

"I. . . I don't know how that happened."

"You don't indeed! Well, I know that at eleven years of age you are responsible for your own clothes, so you will do without that seal pup and a few other pleasures until you have learned your lesson. Do you understand?"

"But Father —"

"Have I made myself perfectly clear?"

"Yes, sir," David replied through watery eyes.

"This proves to me that a boy who is busy with chores does not apply himself to mischief. Now take these smelly clothes below and drop them into a bucket of fat and lye. Perhaps we can salvage them. Away with you!"

Five

*T*he following day rain squalls lashed the ship without let-up. Low clouds hung like a grey lid over the inlet and there was little to cheer the men as they returned from a cold day surveying the shores.

David knocked, stepped carefully over the doorstep and entered the cramped officers' quarters with a tray of roast duck. He placed the platter on the sideboard, served his father first and then passed portions to Mr Perkins, then to Second Officer Wiggins and Fourth Officer Scarfe, a young man of seventeen years on his first long voyage with the Navy. Finally, when Mr Biggs, the ship's surgeon, was looked after, the boy stood back to watch the men eat, resplendent in their white powdered wigs and heavy navy-blue velvet tunics trimmed in fine lace.

"Davie, ask the cook if he has any fresh strawberries. They would go well with the duck, right, Doctor?" Captain Spencer said as he wiped his chin with a silk napkin.

"Indeed they would, sir," the surgeon agreed.

Once the boy had disappeared, Mr Wiggins leaned over towards the captain. "You work that lad too hard, Captain. He's but an infant, you know. Do you think perhaps he's due some time to himself, say for a fortnight?"

The other officers eyed the captain as he stiffened. "Huh," Captain Spencer looked up. "You have no son of your own, I take it, Mr Wiggins? Davie works hard because that is what I expect him to do. He is not a passenger aboard this ship, and he will do his duty as will any other man in this crew."

"Quite right, sir, quite right. Forgive me for bringing the matter up."

"No need, Mr Wiggins," Captain Spencer answered dryly. Then he turned. "Oh, Doctor, have you had a look at Walters' back?"

"Just this morning, sir. The back is healing nicely but I'm afraid his temper hasn't improved. Frankly, Captain, I would put him aboard the first ship heading home, Spanish or English."

Meanwhile, David climbed the narrow staircase from the galley and stepped out onto the deck, cradling a wooden bowl brim full of wild strawberries fresh from the forest. He was about to enter the aft cabin when he noticed three sailors leaning over the rail a few yards off, laughing and making barking noises. He stepped quietly to the edge of the ship and peered down to see his seal pup circling directly below them. One crewman, Walters, held a rusty harpoon while a second tossed small fish into the water.

"No, no, NO!" David shouted. He leaped up and bolted towards the culprit, dropping the berries on the deck as he ran. With a reckless dive through the air, he drove his shoulder into the man's stomach. Both fell headlong to the hard boards in a heap of struggling arms and legs. David drew up onto his knees and, with teeth clenched tight, eyes dancing with anger, he stared into the cruel face beneath him, his fists at the ready.

"Why, you little. . ." Walters muttered as he scrambled to his feet, a hand reaching for the harpoon. "Don't you ever try the likes of that again, I warn you! I'll give you what's coming to you. Just you wait."

David managed to stand up in one swift motion. "Well, if you touch that seal pup you'll. . . you'll swim home!" he shot back, his face beet-red and his two feet dug hard into the boards.

It took a few seconds for the three sailors to recover from their surprise, giving David enough time to make his way back to the galley for a second try with the berries. The two crewmen glanced at Walters and laughed until they almost dropped in their tracks while their fuming victim leaned on the rail, playing aimlessly with his ivory-handled knife, poking it into a wooden peg.

"Laugh if you will, mates, but that makes two Spencers who ain't going to last this voyage." He pointed the knife in their direction. "You mark me words. . ."

The laughter stopped.

Below, in the officers' mess, an impatient captain tapped his fork handle on the tablecloth. He eyed his son coldly as he entered with the wooden bowl, but he said nothing. David felt the quiet in the room, the four officers silently eating, looking neither left nor right.

"May I go now, Father?"

"Huh? Oh, right, right. I'll look after the wine. You can run along. Get to your studies, young man, once you have eaten."

"Thank you, sir."

"Be sure to take sauerkraut with your dinner, Master David. Keeps the scurvy away, you know," the doctor called after him.

He sprinted up the steps, the very thought of sauerkraut

nearly causing him to retch. After a quick look about for his seal pup, he ducked down the fo'c's'le hatch into the gloomy chamber where Grimsbey waited for him at the long narrow table.

"Well there, laddie. You be a mite late tonight."

"I know, Grimsbey. I . . ." He leaned closer to the old man. "I want to talk to you sometime."

Grimsbey helped David to a slice of red salmon, some wild leeks and a chunk of mouldy bread, green spots spreading over the blackened crust. At least the water was fresh, the giant cask having been cleaned and refilled that morning. The quarters were empty, not a soul lying about on his bunk or in any of the ten hammocks strung across one end of the crowded living area. The old man shuffled over to the mast-post to find a candle. He spoke as he worked the flint.

"It's about Walters, isn't it, lad?"

David swallowed a mouthful of bread. "I don't know about him, Grimsbey. Three times now he has given me trouble. First, I know it was him who pulled up the ladder when I was swimming. I know he ruined my best clothes on purpose, and, just tonight, I caught him trying to harpoon my seal pup."

"Aye, he's a no-good loafer. No good at all. Best you keep clear of him. Aye," Grimsbey said as he rubbed his beard. "Have you told all this to your father?"

"Well, no . . ."

"And why not, I ask you?"

"I can't, Grimsbey. Father says I must fight my own battles."

"That's right noble of you, laddie, until the day you come face to face with a battle which is too much for you. The likes of this Walters now, you cannot handle his kind by yourself, you know. Don't you even try!"

"I knocked him down a few minutes ago."

"What? Bowled him over?" the old man frowned.

"When he was trying to kill the seal. I just ran into him as hard as I could. He landed on his back with me on top of him. He was sure mad!"

Grimsbey tugged at his chin whiskers and closed his eyes. "From now on, keep close to your father or to the officers, or me, for all of that. I should say so. If matters thicken, I'll speak to your father meself. Now, eat up if you want to grow up to be a man the likes of the captain."

Six

*D*avid blinked his eyes and sat up. Something had startled him awake. Then he heard three loud knocks on the door.

Still half asleep, he jumped down off the high bunk and stumbled across the floor to the door. His father snored gently under his covers on the opposite side of the great cabin. The boy pushed the brass doorplate free to stare into a pair of black-brown eyes.

"Begs your pardon, young Spencer, but there be Indians off our port bow. Three canoe full of 'em." It was Havlock.

"What's that, Davie? What's the problem there?" Captain Spencer yawned as he spoke.

"Indians, Father! Havlock says they're off the port bow."

"Come in, Havlock," the captain called as he lifted his long coat off its hook. "How many are there?"

"A good twenty and some, sir."

"Are they armed?"

Havlock's eyes widened. "With spears and bows they be armed, sir! Some of 'em have stone knives."

"I'll have a look. Davie, stay put down here."

"But. . ." the boy began to plead, and then, "Yes, sir."

Captain Spencer bounded up the stairs ahead of Havlock, pulling his coat about his shoulders as he went. David was left to see what he could from the great windows sternside, and he wasn't to be disappointed. Before he could settle down on the high bunk, a long narrow canoe glided towards him on the rain-speckled water. It was a sleek craft, about thirty feet in length and under three feet wide, he thought. Its enormous curved prow thrust skyward, red cedar fashioned in the shape of a giant bird with mighty wooden wings outstretched from its thick body. Behind this strange statue stood a man draped from head to toe in a roughly woven cape, his head almost hidden beneath an upturned straw hat. He must be the chieftain, David thought. As the canoe drew nearer, the startled boy caught sight of long wooden spears lying lengthwise across the plank seats within close reach of the eight paddlers who rested quietly in single file.

Through the grey drizzle, David could now see the frightening faces of the visitors, their tawny skin hidden by streaks of red and black paint daubed from their foreheads to their round flat chins. Each strange mask was made even livelier by large piercing eyes which darted back and forth, following the movements of the chief, who was now waving his red cedar cape as if he were a bird himself.

A closer inspection, necessarily swift as the canoe began to slip out of sight around the stern, revealed to David baskets of fresh pink salmon, berries and leeks, all cushioned between large bundles of wet furs bound in twine. Before he could see more, the tip of the canoe disappeared.

This was too much for him to bear. He quickly opened the cabin door and crept up the steps just high enough to gain a decent view of the deck. His father stood amidships at the top of the rope ladder, draped in his great Navy coat and capped by the wide-brimmed hat David sometimes put on when he was alone in the cabin.

Captain Spencer was soon face to face with the swarthy chief who had managed to heave himself up onto the wet boards. Once safe, the guest turned to motion his followers aboard. Then he swung about, pulled his robe over his shoulder and bowed. He was rapidly joined by all twenty-eight of his warriors, each one loaded down with baskets of welcome food. David was surprised by his father's calmness and by the absence of any sign of the ship's guns or side arms.

The rain-soaked chief gave a signal to his men and they obediently squatted on the deck in a ragged circle. All eyes followed him as he slowly withdrew a small basket from beneath his robe. He held the beautifully woven container out towards Captain Spencer, who took it, nodding as he did so. The *Langley's* officers and men moved closer as their captain untied a thin leather thong and raised the reed lid. He reached in and grasped a large rock about the size of a man's fist. David craned his neck to catch a better view of the strange offering.

The doctor stepped forward and adjusted his monocle, curious to find out what such a gift might yield. He scraped a bit of earth away with his pocket knife and, with the help of the pelting rain, managed to clear off a small portion revealing a drab yellow metal. Perkins was the first to speak, in a low gasp. "Gold, Captain. That is a solid gold nugget!"

"A gold nugget indeed," the doctor exclaimed in a hushed voice. "Worth a goodly fortune!"

Captain Spencer's mind was not wholly on the treasure that lay in his open hands. Instead, the ship's master carefully scanned the watering mouths of the crewmen as they eyed the prize, an answer to their very prayers. He wished for all the world that they had not been present to witness the find. Just knowing that there was gold to be had so easily was more than some of them could handle. What was done was done, however, and it now became the added duty of the captain to be more alert than ever.

A few of the natives returned to their canoes, which were moored at the foot of the ladder, and reappeared with the fur pelts and bright red slabs of salmon meat. These treasures were exchanged for pots and pans which clanged as they were jostled down the side of the *Langley*. Finally each one of the officers was warmly hugged by the chieftain, and, as orderly as they had boarded, the visitors climbed down to their three narrow craft and were away in the mist, the ship's company not stirring until they were out of sight.

After a period of impatiently listening to the rain striking the oiled teak, Perkins broke the peace, asking Captain Spencer, "What do you make of that? Jolly decent chaps, weren't they?"

"I should say so, Mr Perkins," the captain answered as he looked in the direction of the vanished canoes. "However, our mission here is to complete a survey, not prospect for gold. We will leave that pleasant duty for other expeditions."

Grimsbey stepped forward to better inspect the large raw nugget. "You never can tell, sir," he said finally.

"What's that, Grimsbey?"

"Well, sir, them natives there, sir. They seemed to be a fine lot, but there be others about, aye. It's best to keep a weather eye out, which is what Captain Cook himself used to say, if you'll pardon me, sir."

"Oh come now, Grimsbey. Those fellows were as friendly as could be. And I don't recall that we had any real problems this far north on Vancouver's voyage."

"As you say, sir," Grimsbey answered. He knew well the law of the sea, and the captain's word was final. He changed the subject. "Wonder the Spaniards aren't hereabouts in tens, hunting for the gold."

"I'm sure they would be if they knew there were nuggets this size for the taking. Doctor, I think we should get out of this rain." The captain motioned the physician to follow him to his cabin astern. It was not the rain, but the hungry eyes of the crew from which he sought shelter. They were edging closer and closer to the valuable rock, their mouths fairly drooling as they eyed the yellow surface. David saw his father and Mr Biggs approaching and shot down the steps to the great cabin. In seconds the two men entered. Once Captain Spencer had carefully bolted the oak door, he placed the rock on the chart table. David rose from his bunk and moved closer as his father and the doctor bent over the treasure. The surgeon began to probe its surface while the captain held it firmly in both hands.

Above them, high on the aft deck above the cabin, three sailors huddled behind the helm, pondering their own possible good fortune. Walters squatted on his haunches, his knees poking through his tattered canvas trousers, a hand-sewn garment strung to his waist with strands of hemp. Tattoos mottled his chest, blue skulls and seabirds marred by deep scars earned in a dozen bloody fights. Skinny Havlock stooped next to him, a man half Walters's size, his thin head sheathed in long black hair swept back and braided into a ratty tail that hung to his belt. His sharp, prominent nose gave his face the beaky look of a parrot. He sported a collection of necklaces, all strung at odd angles around his neck, and long silver earrings stretched the lobes of his ears with their weight. His pants were cut off at the knees, and a tarnished pair of high black boots covered his scrawny shins.

Link was the strangest bird of the threesome. Only five feet tall, he was perhaps twenty years of age, at least five summers younger than either Walters or Havlock. His clothes were ill-matched, from hair to boots, a common sight among thieves. A minister's frock draped his shoulders, a blacksmith's trousers ballooned from his waist and a pair of once-fine shoes, fitting wear for a man of commerce, shod his feet. This wardrobe covered a wasted skeleton almost free of muscle, and it was topped by a humorous face with a gap-toothed grin and a black patch over one eye.

All three men had plans for the magnificent gold nugget and many more like it. They talked in hushed voices, nodding avidly and sometimes slapping each other on their backs in their enthusiasm. Their plan was simple enough and, as Walters put it, "foolproof 'til the end."

Seven

*F*our cutters lay quietly alongside the *Langley*, their oars shipped and survey stores stowed high in the bows. Captain Spencer stood on the quarter-deck reading the day's watches in the dim light of early dawn.

"Mr Perkins will stand watch aboard ship. Mr Wiggins and the doctor will take the first cutter to the east wall of the inlet and I will chart the western shore. Mr Scarfe, you will row farther up the sound and survey the small islands thereabouts, and the bosun will cover the high point where I suspect a river will be found. That leaves three men on board to clean up, Mr Perkins?"

"Correct, sir."

"Which boat will I join, sir?" a small voice piped up.

"The *Langley*, young fellow! There is not much to do out there and you'll only add weight for the rowers. Best you stay put until the survey is done. We'll see after that."

Grimsbey was about to speak up when he saw the expression that fell over David's face, but he chose to keep silent.

Certainly no one wanted Walters, Havlock and Link aboard his cutter, and that left no choice but to post them aboard the big ship for the day. Now David and Perkins would be left alone with them, and Grimsbey couldn't help wondering if something might happen.

In a single command, the tars scrambled down the lines, digging bare toes into the *Langley's* hull, and hopped eagerly into the cutters. The officers and Grimsbey followed, and Number Three boat pushed away, levelling her oars on the water. Two and Four followed, leaving the captain to take one last look about the deck.

"Please, Father, I want to come with you...please!"

"Not this time, Davie. Ah, now...if you're sharp about your chores this morning, you just might swim with your beast for a little bit. But first attend to cleaning up the cabin, the officers' mess and companionways."

"As you say, sir," the boy answered halfheartedly. He turned to watch Grimsbey's cutter move off into the inlet and silently wished that the big man had turned around and asked him to come down and join his crew. He would much rather huddle in one end of a longboat for hours on end than be marooned where he was with Walters and his mates.

David draped himself over the bowsprit, following the white longboats as they weaved along the rock walls of the inlet and finally out of sight. He began to wonder about the Indians and Grimsbey's tale about the three sailors who had disappeared, but Perkins's voice broke his spell.

"Link, you good-for-nothing jackal, you'll not spend your time lolling about here. Get to that line at once! I want splices in all sections by noon. You, Havlock, take your leave and come with me. We will fetch gunpowder and set it smoking to fumigate the fo'c's'le. The place is crawling with fleas and other vermin."

The officer began to stride across the deck towards the forward hatch, then pulled up short. "And speaking of vermin, where is Walters?"

"He's minding the helm, sir. Changing the glass over the compass, sir," Havlock droned.

"Very good. Come along."

Perkins led the way down the forward hatch and through a long series of passageways, dodging dusty barrels and low beams in the darkness. He pulled at a ring of keys strung to his waist and selected one which easily opened the ammunition stores. Just as he was about to lift a small keg from a shelf above his head, he suddenly dropped to the floor. Havlock threw a heavy piece of lumber to one side, snatched the keys from the unconscious man's belt and found his way back up onto the deck.

He glanced about and then called out to Link and Walters. "Ahoy, mates. Mr Perkins would have us down below on the double there."

David followed the antics of the disgruntled Walters as he threw down his tools and wandered as slowly as he could towards the steps. Link remained seated until Havlock gave him a swift kick. "Hurry up. We mustn't keep His Majesty waiting."

Once below the first landing, Havlock cornered the other two and sat them down on a bench. "Hold it now. We've done the deed, we have!"

"What are you talking about, mate?" snapped Walters.

"We've done in Perkins, that's all. He's lying in a lump down in the munitions chamber. He's out for a fortnight. Keys too, see?" Havlock gave a toothy grin and held up the key chain.

Walters reached out and snatched the lot from his friend, staring angrily at him. "That's a stupid move!" he shouted.

And then, remembering that David was not far away, he lowered his voice. "Now why, I ask you, did you do a fool thing like that?"

"Look, when is we going to have a chance like this again? Here we are, us three and one bloomin' officer aboard. And..." Havlock licked his lips.

"And what?" Walters snarled.

"And a hostage such as the kid, right? The captain'll do anything we wants so's to keep his brat alive, now won't he?" Havlock grinned.

"So..." Walters climbed to his feet, a new expression drawn across his face. He stooped to avoid the low beams. "Now here's what we do. Listen up, mates. Best we tie up Mr Perkins in case he comes to."

"I says we takes the boy with us. Do 'em up both at once," Havlock offered.

"I says we don't, right?" growled Walters. "We ain't going to stow both hostages in one place. That would make it too easy for the likes of Spencer and his lot, that would. I'll do the thinking here! Now, come on."

The ship's bell was silent as the noon hour slipped by, the sun at its highest point in the summer sky, beaming directly down on the *Langley*. An eagle spread its wings and floated over the still water, screeching a warning to all below. David watched the beautiful flight as he smoothed a blanket over the high bunk opposite the leaded window. Instead of dusting the cabinet and table, he flopped down onto his father's bed and followed the path of the soaring bird. His gaze wandered to the mirrored surface of the inlet and the perfect reflection of the cliffs on either side.

Suddenly he noticed a rippling in the water and then a familiar head appeared. The boy pressed his nose against the cool windowpane to manage a better view. Then he jumped

down off the bunk, rushed up onto the deck and climbed the
rail post.

"Hello, pup!" he cried. "Here I am!"

The small, round animal poked its silver head high into the
air and barked a salute.

"Wait — I can swim with you today. I'll be right down. I'll
do my chores later."

David looked about for Mr Perkins but the officer was
nowhere to be seen. He bounded down the steps and banged
on his cabin door. No answer. I *do* have permission to swim,
he thought. Without further delay, he flew into his own
quarters, pulled off his trousers and yanked his shirt and vest
free, ignoring the flying buttons. He leaped back up onto the
deck in three long strides and ran to the rail. The pup was
swimming in small circles, waiting patiently. David perched
carefully on the narrow railing and was about to dive when he
noticed a gull sitting on a boom high up in the rigging. Then an
idea struck him.

Taking hold of the shrouds and placing a bare foot firmly
on the rope ladder, he began to climb until he was high on the
topgallant yard. He found himself among the birds and sea
breezes and as he slid slowly across the guyline beneath the
boom, he chanced a downward glance. The *Langley* seemed
but a child's toy, small enough to keep on the table in his
room. And the water looked as if it were a mile below! David
took a deep breath and leaned out until his feet left the shaky
perch and he soared down through the cool air.

A mass of foamy bubbles marked the spot where he had
been swallowed up in the water and the seal dove to find its
friend. Up they floated, exploding into the sun for a breath
of air.

David paused to sweep the hair from his eyes so that he
could find his bearings. Not a soul watched from the ship and

the inlet seemed deserted. He struck out for the far shore with a powerful stroke, and the seal pup swam along beside him. The two knifed through the water at a steady pace until the pup suddenly dove down out of sight. David took a deep breath and dropped, toes first, until he touched the silty white sand at the bottom of the inlet. Then he crouched, flattened out and began to swim around in the shimmering space, dodging the pup at every turn.

Deep in the *Langley*'s bilge, just above the keel, three men wrestled with a length of heavy rope until they were completely satisfied. In the midst of a dozen knots and loops lay Mr Perkins, firmly trussed, with his scarf bound tightly between his teeth to prevent him from calling out, should he awaken.

"Let's get back up topside and find the boy afore he gets suspicious," Link suggested cautiously.

"No hurry. Take it easy. We don't want to surprise him and get him upset, so's we have to knock him out. Wouldn't like to do him in afore we's ready."

"Got to give it to you, Walters," Link replied with a shake of his head. "You be the fine one."

"Aye, mate, you're right about that. Now let's set a spell and get our wits about us."

A quarter mile away, two sea urchins dove and hid among the smooth rocks off the inlet shore. The boy tugged at the seal pup's fin, the little animal submerged and resurfaced and the game started all over again. They churned over the surface and worked their way along the cliff walls until the *Langley* was a mere speck in the distance. After a long sunbath on a sandy beach, they rolled into the lukewarm water and made off for the next small bay, continuing their games as they swam.

First, the boy stood chest-deep in the water and called the seal over to him, holding a small crab above its shiny head. Once within reach, the pup almost danced on the surface until it was able to take the morsel into its mouth. David held up his hand, counted all five fingers and dove for another crab. Coaxing the pup over his shoulder was the next stunt, the small beast swimming over at first and, as David gradually stood up, leaping higher and higher until its body was almost out of the water as it flew by the boy's ear. Whirling around David's knees was an easier stunt, the seal following a piece of clam meat held out in front of its nose. Around and around they went until the boy became dizzy. The pup followed him out of the water and onto another narrow sandy strip. The boy laughed aloud as he watched the seal flop about on the warm stones. "You may be better than me in the water, but I've got you beaten on land." The boy dropped down on the sand and stretched full length on his stomach. The seal came up beside him and nestled against his ribs.

"Look in the cabin again, Link!" Walters cried.

"I already done the cabin three times!"

"Well, the little divil's got to be around here somewhere. Well, don't he?" Walters returned angrily. "Get in there and turn the place upside down 'til you find him."

Havlock climbed down from the helm where he had been scanning the shoreline nearest the *Langley*. "He ain't over there and he ain't swimming around the ship."

"I still say he's in there swimming somewhere, 'cause his clothes is all over the floor down there like I told you," whined Link from the top of the hatch.

Walters ran his tongue across his lower lip. "Get me Perkins's glass!" he growled at Link.

"Aye, now there's thinking for you." Link's eyes brightened. "Perkins's glass she be, mate."

Link hurried below and then back up onto the deck, First Officer Perkins's spyglass in his fist. He raised it to his eye.

"Gimme that!" Walters growled as he snatched the glass from the startled seaman. He hoisted the cylinder to his own eye and scanned the opposite shore. "Huh...ah...no..." Then, after a long pause, "Ah...there! There he be!"

"I told you he wasn't aboard," Link gloated.

"Pipe down and get the skiff ready there."

"Aye," Havlock leaped up.

"We're taking us on a little journey over there to shore, we are," said Walters. "Help him with the skiff, Link."

Havlock stopped short. "Aye, and what are you going to do while Link and me is lugging this here skiff about?"

Walters bristled. "You questioning me, Havlock?" he snarled through clenched teeth.

"No, no, mate. No harm done, right?" the other answered, not quite so boldly as before.

Walters muttered to himself as the round field of the spyglass centred on the boy who was now perched high and dry on a rough granite rock, the seal beside him.

"We lower the boat over the port side so's the lad won't spot us, right?" Link asked.

"Aye, and be quick about it. I can see canoes making way about a mile up the coast there. Two of 'em, maybe more. We don't want to share our hostage now, do we?" Walters said as he continued to peer through the long scope.

"Is they Indian canoes?" Link wondered aloud.

"They ain't Spanish, you idiot!"

"Well, you can count me out of this, if you don't mind, mate!" Link shuddered.

"What?" Walters bellowed. "Lower that boat and be in it afore I fold this here glass or I'll skin you alive!"

Link stared at Walters as he shoved the small skiff to the rail. Havlock helped him ease the line through the pulley in deadly silence.

None of them uttered a word as they sat huddled in the eight-foot-long rowboat, even after they had pushed away from the *Langley*. All three held their eyes on the far shore instead, keeping track of the two high-prowed canoes that sped across the inlet, as silent as a pair of water snakes, inching their way towards the boy and the seal dozing in the hot sun.

Eight

*D*avid shut his eyes to the glaring sun while the seal pup scratched an itchy flipper, trying to coil around to see what he was doing. The little animal cocked its head towards him and watched him through bleary eyes. Then it raised its body up onto stubby fins and slid along the rock into the crystal clear water, surfaced and dared the boy to follow. David climbed to his feet and was poised for a long shallow dive when he glanced around to his right and caught sight of the advancing canoes no more than a few hundred yards off. He was not the least bit frightened, having already encountered the friendly natives aboard the ship. He stood upright and waved to let them know he welcomed their visit.

Out in the skiff, an argument had just come to an end and the wobbly craft was being hastily turned about for a short run back to the *Langley.*

"I still think we could chase 'em off. They didn't put up a

fight on deck last morning," Link fretted. "They'd be afeared of a gun if they never put their ear to one afore."

"And if they's heard a shot or two afore, Link, we'd be sitting ducks for a good dunking, I'll tell you! Anyway, yonder canoes be a bigger boat by far than the tubs they were floating around in t'other day!"

"They's a different tribe, maybe," Havlock suggested.

"Maybe so, but I'm not one to go over there and ask 'em. Come on, let's get up and pull the boat!" Walters replied.

David waited to greet the canoes, now no more than a hundred feet away. He was startled to see that each paddler's face was hidden behind a red cedar mask with large hollow eyes and a wide, gaping mouth. A few warriors wore small capes over their shoulders and others bore clumps of seaweed around their necks. David realized with a sudden chill that, unlike the noisy visitors to the ship, these men were silent. All that could be heard was the even *slup, slup* as the paddles grazed the water.

At an unseen signal, all the men lowered their paddles as one and picked up long spears, standing at the same time. They all stared straight ahead through the gaps in their hideous masks, perfectly motionless. When the closer of the two craft approached David's rock, a tall man climbed to a raised platform at the bow and poised until he was above the stunned boy. In a flash he leaped down, landing squarely on the granite, and reached out to grasp David's arm. The boy turned swiftly around and with a vigorous thrust of his legs dove headlong into the water and began to swim as fast as he could.

The men in the second canoe stood still as they moved towards the English boy, not a word spoken or a hand raised. A heavy-bellied native at the bow of his giant log craft stared down at the doomed quarry and, with a single quick movement, whipped a strange hooked spear in the boy's direction. Just as David lunged out into a crawl stroke, he felt a sharp pain in his arm that stopped him immediately. He had been caught in a bone fishtrap wedged tightly around his upper arm, rendering escape impossible. Once the hooks had surrounded the tender flesh, the spear was pulled back with a jerk and the needlelike prongs tightened around David's arm. The boy writhed in agony, falling limp. He was pulled closer to the massive canoe and a vine noose slipped around his neck, loose enough to permit only a shallow breath.

He fought the pull of the vine cord but every movement sent a bolt of sharp pain down to his fingertips. He was drawn to the side of the slowly moving hull and yanked up like a subdued fish. After he was dropped to the rough flooring, the paddlers lost no time in getting the log craft under way, leaving the boy lying helplessly and painfully alone, shaking with fear. A smelly twine fishnet was draped over him and he was prodded onto his back by a heavy foot.

His first thought was to call out to Mr Perkins or the three sailors, but then he remembered how far he had swum from the *Langley*. Next, he wondered whether the canoes might pass by one of the survey cutters. If they were close enough, he could call out to his father, Grimsbey or one of the officers. They could rescue him, he was sure of that. Before long, however, his thoughts settled upon his sore arm, which was now pounding and swelling. He worked at the terrible hooks, gritting his teeth to master his pain, always keeping an eye out for the paddler sitting above him. Carefully, slowly, he worked the savage hooks loose enough to slide over his wrist. Once free of them, he lay back exhausted, confused, sick and afraid. No thought of his seal pup entered his mind as he settled, cramped and shivering, in his twine prison.

Less than a mile across the sunny water, behind a rocky out-cropping, several British seamen eased their longboat into shore, Grimsbey signalling the others to keep silent. Only moments before, they had spotted the swift canoes and, after counting the number of paddlers, had elected to stay out of sight rather than chance an impossible fight. They squatted low on the beach, the great bearded sailor occasionally peering out, until finally the Indians disappeared.

What might have been another two hours slowly went by, and now David could feel his skin burning under the mid-afternoon sun. To protect himself, he made an effort to roll over onto his side but, without so much as a grunt of warning, a calloused foot sent him sprawling. After that David remained perfectly still. Later, the cliffs shut out the sun, plunging the vessels into cool shadows as they moved through a narrow channel. Once they were clear of the small opening in the rock wall, the sunlight beamed down again on the two long dugouts. On and on they swept over the still waters of a hidden inlet, paddles swinging in perfect time.

David ran his hand down his ribs and over his damp leggings. He wondered how he could be running with perspiration and yet feel so cold. He wondered too how long it would be before his father caught up with these kidnappers. Would his longboat be able to find the passage between the cliffs? And, more important, would he bring enough men to handle the Indians?

Then his mind turned to the sudden horrible thought that he might never be found. What if the *Langley* sailed away without him, leaving him to die here on the coast of America? And what plans did these natives have in store for him?

He badly wished to sit up for a moment to see where he was, but the netting wound about his good arm made movement almost impossible. Had he been able to raise himself, he would have seen a small grey head creasing the water a dozen yards behind the canoe, bobbing under every once in a while. Instead, David lay back against the charcoal splinters, staring into the empty blue sky through his twine bars.

Nine

*T*hree frightened sailors jostled each other for a foothold on
the swinging ladder and, after several attempts, found themselves high and dry on the ship's deck. They cursed the Indians
for making off with their prize hostage and wondered what
they would do if the captain turned out to be willing to trade
Mr Perkins for the life of the ship.

"I told you to lock him up with Perkins," Havlock complained.

"It was me who told him that!" Link protested.

"Aye, well no matter," Havlock continued. "Some leader
you turned out to be, Walters. Methinks your brains be in
your boots."

"Button up, you swine!" Walters snarled as he tightened his
belt. "We got ourselves some three hours afore the survey cutters return to this here barge. Three hours to lay a plan, and
we better have a good one."

The big man ran a hand across his sweaty brow as he
glanced about the sweltering deck. Then, with a lick of his

lips, he waved a finger at his partners and disappeared aft, down the hatch and into the officers' mess. In a moment he reappeared on deck, carrying a full keg of rum over his shoulder.

"First, mates, we raise our spirits with a wee dram of the grog. That'll sharpen our brains." As Walters spoke, he raised the wooden drum and tilted it over his head, his tongue grooved to catch the stream of syrupy red liquor. He gulped a long draft and stopped to breathe before taking a second swig.

The brown cask quickly made its rounds. "Aye, she be a goodly draft, this barrel, mate," Link gasped as he passed the rapidly emptying keg over to Havlock. Then he wiped his mouth on his arm.

"We'll take the ship halfway to Nootka, methinks. That'll give us enough time for the bunch to make up their minds who be with us and who ain't," Walters decided. The barrel was once more his, warmed now by the heat of the scorching sun.

"We'll make Spencer walk the plank! We got ourselves a plank, ain't we?" Havlock managed before a loud hiccup.

"A plank?" Walters repeated as he hung onto the rail. "Everything here's a plank, man. Lot of planks."

"And then that kid of Spencer's'll walk the plank, won't he?" Link slurred.

"Uh-uh," Havlock corrected him.

"And why not?" Link snapped as he clung to a handy line.

" 'Cause, Mr Link, sir, the Indins got him! Remember?" Havlock's eyes began to roll.

"Havlock's right, Link." Walters dropped the empty keg onto the deck. "Methinks we should look for gold right here ...I mean, over there!" He waved his hand towards the shore. "Gimme the spyglass, right?"

"Aye," Link replied and almost fell on his face as he leaned over to Walters with the glass. "I'll get the b-b-boat ready down there."

They toppled over one another in their efforts to ready the skiff, tossing down spare line, copper-rimmed buckets, shovels and spyglass. Link added a musket and two pistols to the cargo. The little boat was loaded almost to the brim and was yet to take on her passengers. Walters ordered Link to climb down the ladder first. Havlock attempted to assist his drunken partner, but he was of no use at all. Instead of easing Link's journey, he managed to lean on him and send him flying into the water. Link popped up to the surface like a cork.

"I — I can't swim!"

Havlock raised his head off the railing and squinted at Walters. "He says he can't swim, Walters."

"I heard him," Walters acknowledged.

"Well. . . what'll we do, mate, sir?"

"Tell him to climb in the boat!" Walters answered, and he grabbed onto the rail to watch this exercise.

As Havlock attempted to refocus his gaze on Link, Walters took to the ladder and fumbled downward until he had one wobbly foot in the skiff. "Made it!" he boasted to Havlock. "Come on, man, try it."

"Whad about Link?"

"Whad about him?"

Just then a loud crash sounded. Havlock had tossed down a full barrel of rum, and it had landed squarely in the centre of the frail craft, causing some of the floorboards to split. Now a stream of water surged up from the sea, causing Walters to fall to his knees, a better position from which to organize his next move. Havlock leaned over the rail and, in three missteps, joined the beleaguered Walters in the sinking boat.

"Push away, matey!" Walters ordered gleefully.

"Whad about Link?" Havlock cried as he hung on, both eyes glued to the water rising to his waist.

As the small boat edged away from the *Langley*, it slowly settled into the small inlet until its gunnels met the surface. There it floated as will all wooden craft, the three sodden sailors hanging on to it, Link having been inspired to swim the few feet necessary to save his life, at least for the time being.

Ten

The sun's rays no longer beat down on David's sore, stiff
body as he lay in the twine fishnet. It was now late afternoon
and the paddlers, apparently tireless, continued their steady
rhythm. Suddenly, every native voice rose into a high-pitched
howl. Silence followed for a moment and then a second shout
wafted over the water from some distant source. Had David
been able to peer out over the canoe's high gunnel, he would
have spotted a village tucked away at the head of the quiet
inlet, smoke rising up from a dozen fires.

The pace quickened, every Indian bending to his work,
paddles whipping across the water. The voices of the warriors
now mingled with the excited cries of the villagers and, in
another few seconds, the boy felt the gravel bottom scrape
along beneath him. With a thud, his canoe halted, causing him
to strike his head against the hard floor.

Shadows crept over him and he twisted about to see what
was happening. He found himself staring blankly into a
spinning mass of dark eyes, their owners leaning over him as

they stood knee deep in the shallow water. The noise was overpowering, a chattering and clucking with scarcely a breath being taken. The faces were of young boys and men, athletic in appearance and all evidently frightened by what they beheld. But they could be no more shaken than the crumpled, bruised boy who lay helplessly before them. Numb, exhausted through and through, David closed his eyes and awaited his fate.

The heavy net was pulled off the shaking prisoner in one quick tug. He opened his eyes to stare once more into a dozen curious striped faces with long black hair half-covering their foreheads. All of them bore broad smiles, and they talked excitedly as they drank in this strange man-child, white-skinned, golden-haired and clothed in long leggings down to his heels. The villagers had never laid eyes on such a creature before and more than one of them ran a finger down David's cheek as if to make sure he was real. Finally, after this first inspection, a brawny arm descended into the canoe and the calloused hand of one of the paddlers grasped the boy's wrist. In an instant, the shivering, frightened captive found himself sprawling on the warm stones of the beach, a forest of legs towering over him.

A shrill voice rang out from above the shoreline and gradually the crowd pushed back from the prisoner, allowing him a better view of the villagers. His first startling discovery was that the boys, like the warriors who had captured him, wore little or no clothing at all. The girls and women were draped in rough capes made of woven cedar strips hung loosely over their shoulders. A few men were decked in dried seaweed aprons while others were adorned with great clumps of ragged weed from head to toe. These people seemed shorter than the crewmen on the *Langley*, David thought, and all of them appeared somewhat alike because of the red and black paint that was smeared thickly on nearly every face in the throng. If he had known that the colourful mixtures were daubed on just for his arrival, he would have been even more frightened than he was.

A husky boy about his own age came forward and poked him with a stick. David drew back, causing the crowd to break into a gale of laughter. Another daring fellow, much older than the first, threw a handful of pebbles which struck him on his face and neck. A third was about to do likewise but was interrupted by a loud beat from a flat drum. Immediately the growing mob fell silent. David could hear the pounding of his heart against his sore ribs, throbbing almost in time with the drummer, and he perched himself on one elbow, trying to see what new surprise swept the attention of the gathering away from him. Suddenly the crowd parted and through the newly formed passage strode an old, bent man, half-hidden beneath a lengthy, feathery white blanket, his face deep brown against his silver-grey hair. He stopped at the boy's feet and, with failing, deep-set eyes, looked long into his face. He ran a gentle hand across David's pale cheeks and mumbled as he studied this exotic golden-haired youth. After what seemed an endless time to the terrified captive, the ancient man stepped back and lifted his arms into the air. All eyes followed his noble gestures and again the villagers fell silent.

"Hiiieeeee!" the faltering voice cried out.

The villagers sank down on the hard pebbles, squatting knee to knee, elbow to elbow. They watched the old man as he waved his hands over David's head. The boy gazed up into his penetrating eyes and prayed earnestly that his life would be spared. Unlike most of the onlookers, this man seemed kindly and thoughtful, his withered hands gentle. The boy guessed that he was the chief and hoped that he might send him back to the *Langley* now that everyone had seen him. At this thought, he returned the warmth of the old native by holding his hand out to him. Suddenly, amid the growing chatter came a hoarse bellow, followed by pushing and shoving that sent some of the smaller children closest to David sprawling on top of him.

The bewildered prisoner pushed himself higher to gain a better view, but he quickly fell back as a giant, heavy-bellied man stomped into the clearing and, without warning, thrust a long spear into the pebbles inches from David's feet. He began to talk quietly to the old man, but his voice gradually grew louder and angrier until he was screaming down into the withered face. As the one-sided argument of clucking and coughing noises grew more heated, the two men backed away, drawing the crowd along with them, leaving some space around David. Soon he found himself alone save for a powerful-looking native spearman standing off a few feet, his eyes fixed on the trembling captive.

Now, for the first time since his arrival, David was able to see the village itself. A wide beach followed the curve of the small bay at the inlet's end, and a few yards from the pebbly shoreline stood a row of wooden houses, their sides lined by vertical planks painted with colourful dyes in artful shapes of animals and fish. Their roofs swept up gradually to low peaks, perhaps two storeys from the ground, their height, however, no match for the tall totem poles guarding each entrance. These massive tree trunks rose into the sky overhead, each one stripped clean of its branches, its bark shorn away and figures of animals carved deeply into the cedar fibres, painted in rich blacks, reds and whites. Each pole was topped by the long, protruding beak of an eagle, and a few boasted eight-foot-long wings spread out on either side.

Behind the longhouses, the forest reared up against the steep rock face of a mountain, a massive granite wall that offered protection from every possible direction except the water. Between mountain and shore there was a scattering of grass beside well-worn, shell-strewn sand paths that criss-crossed each other at odd angles. Beyond David's hearing, the two men who had first caught his attention continued their noisy discussion. It seemed to him an unfair match, this feud between an enormous, muscular giant, perhaps in his thirties, and a thin wisp of a man almost twice his age. He was puzzled too by the daring of the younger man as he addressed his "chief" in such a bold manner. No officer or tar on the *Langley* would chance such a shouting match with his father. Had he questioned his own thoughts, he would quickly have recognized that the younger man was himself chief after all. But for the moment he just watched the two as they argued in a language like no other he had ever heard.

"He *is* the Spirit Child!" the old man was insisting in his sharp dialect.

"I say he is not. I, Tuklit, have spoken!" The huge Indian picked up his spear and thrust it into the ground. "I am chief. You are my shaman, and that is all your power."

"Yes, I am shaman, my Chief, and it is my duty to speak of the Spirits — the thunderbird, the whale god and the salmon god. I speak with them and ask them to protect our people. I ask them to watch over our village and to bring us good signs —"

"What has this to do with the prisoner?" the chief inter-rupted.

"He has been sent to us as a sign, Tuklit. He is a good sign, for he has the eyes of the summer sky, the hair of the golden rock and the skin. . . of a young seal. He is the Spirit of the Seal!"

"Hah! Everything is a sign to you. Everything is a spirit,"

the chief growled. "That pale child is from the big canoe. Our warriors have seen others like him, even if you have not."

"I warn you, Tuklit," the shaman cried as he shook a gnarled finger in the chief's face, "this *is* a Spirit Child and he must be treated with great honour. If you do not show him kindness, his power will tear this village into two villages. His anger will divide our warriors and send them off like dry leaves on the autumn waters. That is an omen. I feel it."

"We will see what power he has, Shaman. That boy from the big canoe shook like a speared salmon when I stood before him. Is that his power?"

"I dreamed there would be a visitor to our village," the old priest continued as if he had not heard Tuklit's question. "I dreamed that we would see many days of harvest, baskets of wild berries, canoes full of giant fish, the forests filled with creatures for our feasting. And all of my dreams have come true, my Chief. You cannot deny that."

The heavy-fisted Tuklit tossed his head from one side to the other in disgust. "Your ways are old, Shaman. They are foolish. I am going to take the boy-child as my slave. He has no blood, but hard work will make him strong. That is my answer to your Spirit talk." Then, turning away from the old man, "Fetch me the prisoner!" he cried.

David was watching the two men as they drew apart and did not see his guard come up behind him. He was yanked onto his feet and led to the longhouse, a strong hand gripping his neck. He passed among the still-curious crowd, feeling the dark eyes staring at him, the boys his own age grinning from ear to ear, reaching out to him with long sticks. An old woman pinched his arm and was sent sprawling by a painted warrior. A little girl, no higher than his elbow, sent a pebble flying and it struck his cheek. He winced, and the older girls and boys laughed. Finally this unhappy march led him to the entrance of the largest longhouse, where he was jerked to a standstill. He chanced a quick look over the inlet, still hoping to see a white longboat from the *Langley* rowing across the water to rescue him. Instead, a single Indian canoe moved quietly over the tranquil inlet, dashing his hopes.

Tuklit stood before David, his feet astride and his thick arms folded over his chest. Behind him collected a cluster of villagers who, the boy imagined, might be his family. There were three young children, a husky boy possibly fifteen years old and an elderly woman, stooped and white-haired. All were silent, eyes glued to the chief, all showing a certain fear of him. At a clucking command, David was thrust forward. He stood shaking in his torn undergarment, perspiration wrung out of him by fear. Tuklit said something to him and the boy shrugged his shoulders and glanced around helplessly. The chief spoke once more, something that sounded like a command. David wished he understood and held out his hands as if to say he could not. Before he could blink an eye, a muscular arm swung out and sent him sprawling onto the grass.

As David reeled back, rubbing his bruised head, the sun slipped behind a heavy black cloud, sending the village into instant darkness. A murmur rose over the surrounding on-lookers and expressions of fear swept over their faces. The old man pushed his way into the clearing and knelt by the stricken boy.

"This is a warning, my Chief. Hear me!"

The shaman reached out and, touching the boy's swelling ear with gentle fingers, he stared up at Tuklit. He spoke firmly, even with his cracked voice, and although David couldn't understand the words, it seemed to him that he was warning the tribe of some danger. Tuklit listened to the shaman for a moment and then, growing impatient, waved him off and ordered the prisoner to be taken into the longhouse. David was shoved with a prodding foot and dragged into the darkness within the cedar building just as the sun reappeared from behind the massive cloud.

Beams of light poured through the small square openings in the roof high overhead and struck the cedar pillows, making it difficult for David's eyes to penetrate the darkness beyond. Gradually, though, standing near the middle of the structure, he became accustomed to the searing columns of brightness and began to see more clearly the awesome size of this strange house. The floor beneath his feet was earthen, the hard surface covered by a layer of soft dust. The centre portion of the great hall was bare except for three fire pits, the closest to him still spitting sparks from red embers. He guessed the floor to be a hundred feet long and at least fifty feet wide, larger by far than the *Langley*. From either side of the chamber, walls jutted in towards the centre, creating private compartments for many families, each unit open to the hall, where people might gather about the fire pits. High wooden benches or shelves lined the smaller areas, all spilling over with furs, baskets and other possessions.

The boy raised his eyes and followed the long wooden beams that spanned the length of the ceiling. The narrow crosspieces, which must have been at least twenty feet above the heads of the tallest warriors, now proved to be a handy perch for young boys his own age to lie about on, their legs dangling in the air, their heads flopping over the sides as they listened to their elders. David took his eyes off them long enough to glance at the two tribal leaders, still arguing, but now joined by at least a dozen older men and women. Nearby, a pair of boys wrestled each other over a large animal bone of some kind, throwing one another about on the hard ground and thumping fists on bruised bodies as if they had never heard of pain.

An old woman shooed them away with her foot and returned to the centre fire pit to stir some stew bubbling in a
massive wooden bowl carved in the shape of what David
thought looked like a killer whale. He could smell boiling fish
and hear it sizzling as more white-hot rocks were ladled into
the pot to cook the tender morsels through and through. A
matted robe covered the woman from shoulders to ground,
and two babies crawled under the long reed gown one at a
time to hide from one another.

Every so often, the wooden panels covering the entrance
would ease open, allowing still more villagers to clamber in to
have a look at the strange, pale slave boy. Some were very
fearful of David, jumping back quickly when he moved even a
hand. Others simply stood quietly, well back, pointing to him
as they whispered.

Tuklit towered over the fire, now kindled into a roaring
open-air furnace, his face aglow in the brilliance of the flames.
He shouted over the crackle and sputter, causing the visitors to
abandon David and gather about the fire pit to share the salty,
savoury dishes. The boy's stomach growled as he sniffed the
aroma of roasted oysters, clams and freshly broiled salmon
served with wild red strawberries. He tried to remember when
he had last eaten and wondered if he would be included in the
feast set before his eyes. He waited patiently, listening to the
endless clucking of voices and the laughter of children. He
watched a tame raven gobble up tidbits of salmon thrown to it
by the younger boys and was saddened as the last of the food
was set aside on shelves along the wall across from him. He
began to feel very lonely and his elbow, badly torn by the ugly
fish hooks, was now puffed and throbbing, the pain slowly
creeping up towards his shoulder.

Darkness stole the last remaining flicker of daylight and the
hungry, terrified boy, unable any longer to stay upright, lay

back against a rough post. At least he was no longer the centre of attention. He listened to the steady chatter of the natives, the old men taking turns telling stories in the fire's glow, stretching their arms out to add power to their legends. As they did so, they drew gasps from the listeners and, more often, bursts of laughter as they screwed up their faces in clownish expressions. Some of their tales caused the younger men to eye each other privately, as if to say they could not believe what they were hearing. The children, however, sat openmouthed, spellbound by every word. For the time being, they were too busy to pester David, and he was grateful for that.

One grizzly man, covered from head to toes in a thick matting of seaweed, snatched a flat drum from a shelf and began to beat mercilessly as he hummed an eerie song. Others joined him, stronger voices that livened the pace as they filled the air, a crying sound which made the English boy shiver down to his bones. Soon young men rose and donned short capes and reed hats. One by one they moved to the centre of the floor in a rapid dance, shuffling bare feet through the dust, eyes tightly closed, each man listening to his own rhythm. A tall, angular native strapped on a pair of enormous eagle wings, six feet of black plumes lined with tufts of white down. He managed to hold the wings aloft as he swooped about the room, daring members of the crowd with his onrushing feet. His swerving and bowing created awesome shadows on the high ceiling.

The music quickened and became such a din it filled every nook and cranny of the flame-lit chamber. Boys David's age moved out of the darkness and began to circle the fire pit, the flames lighting them so that the audience could marvel at their painted skins, blue-black eyes popping and mouths stretching from ear to ear, long, broad stripes down their arms and legs, looking for all the world like giant frogs, the captive boy thought. His guess was quickly proven true when they began their dance, hopping from a low squat, leaping high into the air and landing again on all fours as they croaked a familiar call. David almost forgot his own grim plight as he wondered how they could jump so high off the ground. After the crowd's lengthy applause, they too disappeared into the shadows to make way for a massive figure wearing on its shoulders a magnificent wooden mask whose beak stretched six feet from jaw to tip, a rainbow of colours and finely carved. The children shrieked as it approached them, and even some of the warriors seemed to squirm out of its way in awe of it. The man under the mask worked in short steps in time with the drummers until he finally found a corner where he could rest his weary shoulders.

As the night wore on, families gathered their wandering children, their mats and food bowls, and quietly disappeared. Soon there was only a small handful of villagers left around the fire pit, and an old man poured earth on the smouldering embers of the last remaining fire. Everyone seemed to drift away into the darkness to find his shelf bed and fur blanket. The tired captive's head dropped to one side and, for the moment, he escaped from his prison into a deep sleep.

Eleven

Grimsbey puffed as he heaved himself onto the deck, closely followed by his crew. "She's a dead ship, sir," he said quietly.

"Strange, this. Very strange. Davie! Davie?" the captain repeated. "Mr Perkins?"

"They can't have gone ashore, Captain," Grimsbey surmised. "I'll have a look below, with your leave."

"Very well. Take a few chaps with you. I'll check aft."

The captain turned and glanced down with a start. In the fading light he was shocked to find the deck moistened by a thick, syrupy goo with the unmistakable odour of rum. Kneeling down, he ran a finger through the mess and held it up to his nostril.

"Wiggins, is that you?" he said as he whipped around at the sound of footsteps.

"Aye, sir."

"Is the doctor with you?" Captain Spencer demanded.

"Aye, Captain. Is something amiss?"

"I should think so. There is nary a sign of Davie, Mr Perkins or those three ruffians we left on board. Take your men and begin at the bilge. Search every square foot of this vessel!"

"You heard the captain — look sharp!" Wiggins shouted as he disappeared down the gangway into the fo'c's'le.

Within minutes all three squads were back amidships, Wiggins and the doctor supporting an unconscious and bruised Perkins between them. Captain Spencer had already discovered empty kegs lying beneath the mainmast and Grimsbey had turned up David's outer clothing in the great cabin. His father guessed immediately that David had taken an evening swim, and he set the men to the rails to scan the shores with what light was left to them. It was Grimsbey who dealt the most telling blow.

"After the men tied up Mr Perkins, sir, it looks like they shipped out in the skiff. It ain't in its place forward, sir. The lines are cut and a trail of rum leads to the toprail."

"They must have taken Davie with them," the captain followed, trying to hide his deep concern.

"Maybe not, sir. Begging your pardon, Mr Spencer," Grimsbey replied.

"Oh? Why do you think that?"

"They's not enough room in the skiff for three grown men, let alone four, sir."

"Grimsbey has a point," the doctor said. "Those three scruffy characters couldn't manage themselves, let alone David, with all that rum in their bellies."

"You are saying, gentlemen, that my son is somewhere off by himself? Is that it?"

Suddenly Perkins uttered a low moan and both the captain and the doctor knelt down at once, the others crowding closer. The injured man winced, held up his head for a moment and then lay back once more on the deck.

"I...I am sorry...indeed...I allowed Havlock and his friends to...put me away," the stricken mate gasped.

Captain Spencer took him gently by the collar. "Perkins, my man, where is Davie?"

"I...I'm sorry...I, ah..." Perkins shut his eyes and his head rolled to one side. The doctor placed a hand over the mate's nostrils and then looked up at Captain Spencer.

"He is very much alive, but he can't help us until he is fully conscious, I'm afraid."

"How long will that be?"

"Time will tell..."

"Well, we do not have time, Doctor! We cannot just stand about here — have the men carry him to his quarters." Then, standing, the captain looked about. "Oh, Wiggins! I would ask for volunteers to give search to the shoreline while we still have light."

Before Wiggins could call out, every crewman stepped forward, causing Captain Spencer's face to redden.

"I...I am grateful, all. Mr Wiggins, you will organize the parties. Carry on!"

The captain strode slowly to the starboard rail, pulling his glass from a leather pouch on his belt. He adjusted the eyepiece and carefully scanned the closest shoreline, rock by rock, tree stump by tree stump. Back and forth the foot-long cylinder waved until daylight no longer held. Once the rock and brush melded into a single grey mass, the distraught father pushed himself from the railing and bowed his head. Out on the darkening tide, the longboats plied in and out of the tiny bays until they too were engulfed in the oncoming night.

"He will be found, he must be found!" Captain Spencer repeated over and over to himself. "Oh, I should have left him at home. What made me do this? Why?...why?"

He was roused from his thoughts by the sight of Grimsbey's

boat returning alongside, the crewmen silent as they mounted the flimsy ladder.

"Nothing, sir," the bosun called up to him.

The captain looked down at his hands. They were trembling as they clung to the varnished rail, nails tapping against the polish. He swallowed, took a long breath and gazed out into the darkness. "Where is he? Where is Davie?" he whispered half-aloud. Only the loon replied, its low mournful cry echoing across the black night.

Twelve

*D*avid opened his eyes to squint into a stream of sunlight flowing through the opening in the roof. It took him a moment to realize where he was, and then the sounds around him began to make sense. He could hear the harsh squawk of the raven and the cries of children playing in the shallow water outside. A stone adze clunked against dry cedar and women talked in low voices over the red glow of the fire. He sat his sore, stiff body upright and stretched.

Near him, the chief and his family slept, wrapped in heavy animal skins, sprawled out on the layers of shelves raised off the dirt floor. Before long, a baby began to whimper and the huge man stirred just enough to waken himself. He roused his wife and son, sending them out into the cool morning air to fetch wood for the fire. Then he half-fell from his bed and lumbered across the chamber to examine his new slave. David eyed him as he approached, hunting for a glimmer of kindness in his face. But there was none. The scowling chieftain towered over the young boy, gave him a rude push and then

found his way back to the glowing fire pit. Before long, his
son returned with an armful of bark, closely followed by his
heavily laden mother. The boy flung his wood chips into the
flames and squatted down to warm himself.

The fat-bellied chief scratched his scalp as he watched his
sleepy son. He called him "Klutu" and then rattled off a long
order, pointing to David as he spoke. The sullen youth
climbed to his feet and walked towards the English boy, kicking up a cloud of dust with his toes. Without stopping, he
reached down and, grasping the young captive by the hair,
half-dragged him towards the entrance. David lurched and
stumbled as he tried to regain his feet and, to save himself,
he took hold of the Indian boy's arm. A brown fist swung out
and sent the smaller boy reeling through the opening to fall in
a heap in the bright sunlight.

Quickly "Klutu" pulled David onto his feet and marched
him down to the hot beach, stopping beside a long slab of
driftwood. He took the blond boy's head in his hands and
pushed downward until David's fingers were almost touching the log. Using his one good arm, the frightened boy tried
to budge the heavy timber, but it held fast. This led to
an episode of screaming and kicking which attracted every
youngster within hearing distance. Klutu was now the chief,
all-powerful, brave and clever, and was certainly the centre of
attention as he continued to shout at the English boy. He enjoyed the power he seldom felt, being the unfortunate son of
a brutal father. Now he was chief, and David his slave. He
urged the onlookers to pelt the boy with stones, forcing him to
shield his face, head and swollen arm.

One of the newcomers retreated and reappeared, dragging
a little girl, evidently a slave like David, behind her. Klutu
ordered the little one to lift the driftwood, and she picked
up one end and pulled it slowly up the beach, pushing her robe

to one side as she worked. This was a signal for great mirth, the Indian boys and girls dancing around David, calling him names. Although he could not understand them, he could guess what they meant.

The old shaman, watching from the bluff above the beach, was saddened by what he saw, and not a little worried. He motioned to the little slave girl as she passed by him, and she dropped the timber and followed him to his longhouse. In a short time she returned to the pebbles carrying a wooden bowl filled with berries and pieces of freshly cooked venison. As she neared the other children, the old man shouted something at them and they quickly scattered. Even Klutu ran off, unsure how his father would behave if the shaman were insulted. Now the girl was able to approach David in safety, and she laid the bowl at his feet and stepped back.

Her bright round eyes followed his every move as he tore at the strips of meat and gulped the berries down without chewing them. Once finished, he licked his fingers and hands like a young bear cub. Only then did he realize that he was not alone. He turned his head slowly to look at the girl, only to meet her steady gaze, which embarrassed him. He blinked and looked away quickly, pulling his knees up to hide his filthy leggings. He wondered why she should bring him food, let alone stay beside him. He couldn't be sure she was a slave, for she appeared exactly like any other girl in the village.

David glanced down at the empty bowl, picked it up and turned it over as if to examine it. He passed it to the native girl and she climbed to her feet.

"Ah . . . thank you," he said slowly, even though he knew that his words would not be understood.

"Nootka," the girl whispered.

"Nootka?" David said.

"Nootka," she answered, and her face broke into a broad

smile. She backed away, staring at the flustered boy, re-
peating, "Nootka."

David watched her as she retraced her steps to the shaman's
longhouse. He wondered where he had heard the word
"Nootka" before, and then suddenly remembered.

His father had told him that the *Langley* would visit Nootka
Sound, the most northerly point on the voyage. That was it!
She was from Nootka Sound, and considering the manner
in which she was treated by the village children, she must be
a prisoner like himself. At last, he thought, he might have a
friend who understood how he felt.

David's thoughts were interrupted by a searing blow to his
head. It was the Indian youth again, but this time he did not
have a chance to yank David up by the hair. The English boy
jumped up instead to face his "master," thus saving himself a
painful ordeal. Klutu signalled him to follow and then swung
about to pick his way over the pebbles to the longhouses. The
pair trampled the sharp reed grass and soon found themselves
between two of the barnlike cedar dwellings, the ground under their feet covered with an evil-smelling compost consist-
ing of dried clam meat and human droppings. Once past the
horrible wastes, they reached the rear of the houses only to be
faced with the grim remains of the week's garbage. Flies and
hornets darted about their heads and grumpy raccoons scuf-
fled off into the low bushes. The native boy handed David a
large net and then reached down and scooped pieces of putrid
fish guts into it. He grunted as he wiped his hands on his thighs
and motioned the slave boy into action. David almost gagged
as he bent to his task but swallowed hard until he at last finished filling the swollen twine net with the stinking refuse.
Klutu then signalled him to lift the mess onto his shoulders,
and he wrestled with the weight, unable to budge it. But he was
soon saddled with the heavy burden, Klutu having boosted

the net onto the boy's sagging back. Now his legs wobbled as he tried to follow his escort over the rough path. Blood trickled down his shoulder blades as jagged oyster shells pressed into his tender skin, and the pain brought tears to his eyes.

Klutu moved around behind David and, whenever the pace slowed, the broken slave boy received a sharp swipe over the ankles with a blackberry vine, which only served to make him stumble. Finally, after what seemed an endless winding trail, they arrived at a massive dump, alive with flocks of screaming gulls and cawing ravens, all vying for scraps of rotting refuse. Reeling from the stench, David let the heavy net fall onto the ground with a crunch. He glanced up behind him, only to find that his guard had stopped a few yards back and was leaning restfully on a fallen tree trunk.

Once the great net was shaken empty, the smaller boy swung about to find his way back to the main path. Before he could plant his feet on solid ground, however, he heard a savage growl from just over his shoulder. Whirling around, he found himself staring into the face of a massive brown bear, reared up on its hind legs, its head waving about blindly, paws clawing the air. It sniffed at the man-scent and bared its ugly fangs. David leaped backward, flinging himself to one side as his throat choked a scream into silence. He darted through the prickly bushes, the huge beast breathing at his heels, and lunged over a small log. His foot was caught in a patchwork of bramble that sent him sprawling headlong, his body rolling beneath a wide chunk of dead bark. The enraged bear thundered over the shelter and beyond it, losing track of its quarry completely. Its snarl of fury was enough to loosen the spellbound Klutu from his hiding place and send him down the trail in full retreat. The old bruin picked up this new scent and tore after the native boy, closing on him foot by foot.

The slave boy lay hidden for some time before he dared to crawl from his lair and find his way back to the village. He thought about escaping his tormentors and fleeing through the forest, but this single experience with such a monster was enough to convince him that anything would be better than facing another bear. No, for the time being, he would have to take his chances with the villagers. His mind made up, he struggled from beneath the bark cover and gained his wobbly legs. He was a sad picture, his hair and skin caked with red cedar stain, long scratches showing through his torn and bloodied leggings and his back streaked with deep gashes.

He brushed himself off with his hands as he listened for any hint of the bear or Klutu. Then, satisfied that he was reasonably safe from both of them, he began his unhappy journey back to the village compound. Had he started sooner, he would not have missed the great excitement that stirred the villagers to shouts of praise and wonderment. As Klutu told it, the pale slave boy had faced One-Eye, the bear, and using his magic power, he had made himself disappear completely, leaving One-Eye to claw the empty air!

After hearing his son's story, Chief Tuklit was beginning to wonder if the words of the shaman were indeed true. Could this bloodless child be from the gods? A Spirit Boy? He demanded that his son tell the story over again. As Klutu began to speak, the villagers fell silent, all turning their heads to watch the small, dishevelled figure of the mysterious visitor walk slowly across the compound.

David returned their stares, expecting at any moment to be set upon and beaten mercilessly. Instead, every one of the Indians stood his ground, content to stare at the blond boy in confusion and awe. The old shaman approached him and drew a scrawny arm around his shoulder. David looked up at him as he cried out something in his language. If only he could understand . . .

"Honour him!" the shaman was saying with all the power of his failing lungs. "Honour the Spirit Boy!"

A few of the villagers raised their arms into the air while others stood still, puzzled expressions across their faces. Tuklit remained silent as he watched the shaman whip up the crowd, stirring more and more of the villagers to a fevered pitch of excitement. At last he drew back his broad shoulders, stepped out into the crying mob and demanded silence.

"I, Tuklit, do not call this slave boy a Spirit Child. I see instead that my son is a coward. He told this foolish story to hide his weakness!"

The listeners craned their necks to catch a glimpse of the perplexed teenager as his father continued.

"The slave boy is not special. He is not from the gods. I have spoken!" the chief bellowed as he glared down at his son before turning away, leaving the boy to suffer the taunts and jibes of the younger children. "Klutu will never be chief!" they cried. "Klutu is a coward! Klutu will never be chief!"

David carefully picked his way around the villagers who were now drifting away from the humbled Indian boy. He himself was no longer the centre of attention; that, at least, was something to be enjoyed. He wandered quietly along the shell-strewn path that led to the beach, his swollen feet numb to the pebbles. Each step brought him closer to the soothing water of the inlet, where he hoped he could wade into the lukewarm sea and wash his sore limbs. Once again he thought about escaping as his eyes drank in the stillness of the water which must lead to the outer inlet somewhere beyond the mountain ridge. He found himself searching the shoreline for a white longboat, perhaps for the hundredth time, a magic cutter that would sweep him off to the *Langley*. He stood for a few minutes, a lonely sentinel on the deserted shoreline, waiting patiently for a rescue that was not about to happen.

His attention was broken sometime later by a clicking of shells against the granite rocks to his left. He awakened from his daydream and recognized the girl "Nootka," sitting a few feet from the shore, her hands flying as she cracked the tough shells of fresh oysters against the stones. She poured the soft white meat into a cedar bowl, working rapidly in hopes of pleasing her mistress, who kept watch from the bluff just above the beach. The boy wandered over to her and sat on a rock a few feet away from her. She smiled at him and seemed pleased that he was there. He wished he could talk to her, tell her about himself, ask her how she had found her way to this village. He said "Hello," and she smiled again, her round eyes shining like black diamonds. She held a raw oyster out to him in the palm of her hand, but his stomach turned at the very sight of it. At that moment the old woman growled a warning to her slave and the girl withdrew her hand, much to David's relief. Although he was very hungry, he was not quite prepared to swallow such a slippery, strangely flavoured supper. Nonetheless he was satisfied just to know that he had two friends upon whom he could depend — the old shaman and Nootka.

He thought it wise, for her own safety, to leave the girl to her work, so he climbed to his feet, stretched and then made his way to the edge of the tide and lowered a toe into the salty water gently pushing its way among the barnacled rocks. It was as warm as a bath, and he carefully waded out until he found soft sand beneath his feet. The deeper water was slightly cooler, but it felt like a soothing medicine washing over his torn skin. He was soon waist-deep and he held out his arms as he moved outward, the coolness tickling his ribs.

A soft blow against his knees jarred him alert and he

glanced down into the water to see a silvery shadow darting about. Another gentle push against his leg was enough — he took a deep breath and dove under to meet his seal pup eye to eye. They swam along beneath the surface, bobbing up for air and ducking under once more. They nuzzled each other's noses, then shot forward, twisting and turning in rhythm with each other's movements.

David laughed to himself with joy and the bubbles floated up from his lips, the pup chasing them to the surface. Wondering if the small beast remembered the tricks he had taught it, he dove deeper to pick a blue mussel shell off the sandy bottom. Then he flew up to the surface, glancing around for his friend Nootka. He held the shell up high in the air and called out just in time, for the seal rocketed out of the water and touched the shell with its nose, dropping back into the sea with a resounding splash. The girl laughed at this, and David needed no more coaxing. He signalled the animal with an outstretched arm.

"Come on, jump!"

The round body leaped up out of the water, over the boy's arm and back down again, not once but four times in a row. It swam over his shoulders, first one and then the other. The boy called out to it and it tossed its head. Then the two dove and reappeared, slapping arm and fin against each other, ducking and turning.

As the performance continued, the old woman perched on the grassy bluff put down her weaving and watched, her mouth open wide in amazement. . . and fright. She motioned to two others nearby and soon a small gathering was drinking in the awesome sight of the pair, boy speaking to animal and animal answering boy. How could he do this? How could he talk to the animals if he was not filled with Spirits? And then there was old One-Eye . . .

Before long, the word had spread and the beach became crowded with stunned onlookers. David had no idea he had become the centre of so much attention. He continued to play with the seal, showing off for Nootka to his heart's content. When he had exhausted his stunts, he lay on his back and floated restfully in the sunlight, the seal pup drifting along beside him on the incoming tide. David rolled slightly, and then he saw them — perhaps two dozen natives, all of them staring in his direction, wide-eyed and grimly silent.

Thirteen

Grimsbey paused before the polished oak door, then knocked quietly.

"Come in?"

"Excuse me, sir, but I brought you some soup and a fresh dish of berries."

"Oh, Grimsbey, thank you, but I'm not hungry at the moment."

"Aye, Captain, I expects it's the doctor's business, sir, but we're all a bit worried about your health, sir. It's been all of two days now since you had a meal."

"Has it been that long? My...I have made an error in the log, then. What is the tide?"

"She be real low, sir. A man could almost walk ashore," Grimsbey answered as he walked to the leaded window. "And the sun, she be good to us too."

"Uh-huh. The cutters out?" Captain Spencer asked distantly.

"Aye, sir. Two for the search and two for the survey as you ordered, sir."

The haggard captain rose and moved slowly to the window. He stood opposite Grimsbey, eyes cast to the floor. "My wife," he said in a shaking voice, "my poor wife... It'll be nine long months, perhaps a year, before she hears that she has lost her only child. We had two others who died at birth you know, Grimsbey. A little girl and another boy. It — it just doesn't seem right!" The stricken man turned away to hide his tears. He returned to his chair and slumped down.

"For sure, sir, it ain't fair at all, but none of us have given up hope! Aye, nary a man done that, Mr Spencer, sir," Grimsbey replied gently.

David's father spoke without facing the old man. "This is a ship of the fleet, Grimsbey. We can't remain here forever looking about for a lost soul — and three others at that."

"Aye, sir. Aye." Grimsbey felt a tear well up in his own eye. "If you'll pardon me, sir, I best be getting back to me duties."

"Thank you, Grimsbey."

"Aye aye, sir."

The old sailor stepped out of the dimly lit oak cabin, leaving the dishevelled captain to his own thoughts. He had heard the stories, which Grimsbey loved to repeat — the disappearances, the coastal slavery and worse. He shook his head in his agony, then pushed himself up off his chair. After staring vacantly about the room he walked with an unsteady gait to the window. He recalled once more the pleading of his wife, urging him to leave David home for one more year at least. He recalled his sometimes harsh treatment of the boy and wished he had told him how proud he was of him, how much he treasured him...

On the deck above the lonely cabin, Grimsbey stood beside

Mr Perkins, watching with keen interest the rapid approach of Wiggins's cutter, the slim craft moving at full oar, towing a badly holed skiff behind her. The first officer and bosun hastened to the *Langley*'s ladder.

"We found her topside-up about ten leagues along the inlet!" Wiggins called out. "No oars, no sign of life."

"Were there any Indians in sight?" Perkins demanded.

"Not as we noticed, sir."

"Bring her up, lad!" Perkins shouted. Then he turned to Grimsbey. "Report this news to the captain."

Grimsbey moved off, his mind filled with doubts about whether Captain Spencer need know about this latest find. His heart told him to keep the matter to himself, but his sense of duty sent him down the companionway to face the oak door. He gave himself a moment to gather up courage before he knocked.

Fourteen

*E*very man, woman and child squeezed into the shaman's longhouse, youths hanging from the high beams and babies crawling among a sea of reed skirts. Some of the onlookers heard for the third time the excited words of the old woman and her friends, and none tired as they listened.

"He spoke to the little animal and the small one talked back to him!" one elderly woman repeated.

"It is as she has said," assured another. "It is true. The pale one commanded and the seal obeyed."

"The gods have given us a Spirit Child!" the shaman broke in. "It is as I have said many times. We have been honoured. Our village has been blessed."

Tuklit, shifting from foot to foot, was becoming uneasy, his eyes darting to avoid the stares of his people. After listening for a few more minutes, he stepped out in front of the speakers, holding up a brawny arm for quiet.

"Shaman, if the gods have done as you say, if they have

given us a Spirit Child, then let this Child show us his power. Let the gods tell us to our faces!"

The old man pondered this suggestion for a moment and then raised his bleary eyes. "Very well. It shall be as you say. Come, follow me to the edge of the water and be blessed with the Child's magic."

Tuklit was of two minds as he walked ahead of the swelling throng, and he was growing more frightened by the second. Perhaps the shaman had been right all along. Perhaps the story his son had told was true. As he wondered, he fell behind the crowd hastening towards the shoreline. Arriving last, he satisfied himself with a view from the back row of onlookers.

David had long since left the water and was now sprawled out in the hot sun, drops of salty moisture trickling down the grey granite rock beneath him. The seal pup was circling in the shallows and Nootka was sweeping up the last of her oyster shells into a reed sack. The English boy was pleased with himself: he had proven himself a skilled animal trainer and brought happiness to his new friend. He sat up for a moment to examine the torn skin on his knee. Picking at the ragged strands that had once been his best underclothes, he wondered what he would do when they fell to pieces. He rested his head on his knees as he contemplated his future and then looked up to see what was causing the mounting noise high up on the beach.

No more than a dozen feet away, the first wave of villagers poured down upon him, chattering, buzzing like a swarm of bees. They were led by the wise old shaman, and their faces did not appear unfriendly. No one tossed stones or branches at him. No one threatened him with a fist. The crowd stopped short, leaving a good distance between him and themselves, but the shaman came forward until he stood by the boy's side.

The aged priest bent over, waved his hand above David's head and sang a strange song, his nose almost touching David's, and when he stopped to take a breath, he rested his hand upon the top of the boy's blond head. Finally, he walked to the water's edge and beckoned the boy to follow him. Again he sang, all the time pointing to the calm surface.

For a moment the bewildered boy thought that the old man wanted him to leave the village or even that he wished now to take him back to the ship at long last. But then the shaman approached him again, this time taking him by the hand and leading him to the edge of the tide. Once more he waved his thin arm out over the water. Then he chattered a meaningless command in a gentle voice.

"Huh — they want me to show them how I can swim!" David said to himself. He turned and gazed at the shaman, who was now looking down at his feet. Suddenly Nootka sprang up and pointed to the small animal basking on the boulder a few yards down the beach. The boy's eyes brightened. Now he knew what they wanted!

"Arf, arf, arf!" the boy called out and, in an instant, the seal pup slipped into the water and swam between his legs. "Roll over — come on!" David commanded, and the pup obeyed him at once. "Over my shoulder, boy, over you go." The small seal soared out of the water and dove in over and over again, its warm wet fur skimming past the boy's ear. Then both boy and animal rolled onto their backs, human hands clapping and then seal flippers flapping together in perfect time. All the villagers save Tuklit laughed and cheered. The chief stood alone, mesmerized, shaken deeply by this telling performance. He moved through the throng and caught the old shaman's attention as David waded into deeper water.

"The gods will be angry with me, Shaman. They may destroy me — I have made the Spirit Child a common slave."

"If our songs and dances are strong enough, the gods may forgive you through the Spirit Child. They may forgive all the people of the village. Come, there is much to be done."

The shaman turned to the celebrating throng and bade them be silent. "Now you have seen the magic. Let us welcome the Spirit Child as we should have done yesterday. The Spirit Child shall hear our songs and see our dances! He will receive our thanks for not punishing us all!"

David slid under the surface of the water for the tenth time, followed by the tireless pup. They dove to the bottom of the warm bay and the boy plucked a shell from the sand and swam upward, holding the prize between his teeth. The seal pup did likewise and followed him to the surface.

"This will make them laugh," David thought to himself, but when he cleared the hair from his eyes he saw only the backs of people as they moved hastily up the beach, the chief and the shaman in the lead.

Worried that he might unwittingly have displeased them, David swam ashore and slid onto a smooth rock across from where Nootka sat watching him. He looked into her face for a clue to what was happening, but instead of a smile or a hand signal, she gazed at him as if he were an apparition. Her eyes widened and she rose and carefully backed up the pebble beach, staring at him as she retreated.

David was left alone to ponder his fate for what seemed an hour before he was startled by the sound of pebbles crunching under running feet. Three swarthy warriors, grinning from ear to ear but keeping well back, held their arms out to him. Then one of them reached out carefully and took the boy's hand and motioned him to follow them. Was this going to be the end? David's heart skipped a beat or two and he looked back desperately over the inlet.

In a matter of seconds he found himself before the door of

the chief's longhouse, shaking like a leaf, rivulets of perspiration mixed with salt water streaming down his chest. Suddenly a burst of drumbeats broke the grim silence inside the hall and a hundred natives began to cheer.

David was guided through the small entrance and escorted slowly between row upon row of grinning warriors now painted in ceremonial blacks and reds. Their bodies were streaked with white clay, and feathers decorated their long hair. They faced the boy, smiling and nodding, some singing quietly, all of them keeping their distance, allowing him plenty of room to pass by. As flames rose from the fire pits, he could see the rest of the villagers packed into corners and on shelves, the beams above him crowded with climbing bodies.

The thoroughly terrified boy was finally placed inside a circle of elders who, dressed in magnificent robes, sat around the centre fire pit. Each one uttered low wails, the shaman alone standing now, his head bent back, his withered face towards the ceiling. David thought he must be praying, and he didn't want the old man to stop: if these were to be his final few moments on earth, he wanted them to last as long as possible. But the ancient priest abruptly sat down and the warriors behind the boy began to dance to the drum beats, raising the summer dust to their knees.

In the midst of the thunderous noise made by the dancers came the shrieks of five old women who joined the circle of elders. They took the boy by his shoulders and led him away to a small chamber off the main hall. There they quickly began to tear off his ragged leggings, while he clung to the thick waistband and resisted with all his might. The women gave up this first mission and proceeded to daub a smelly fish oil over his bruised skin, leggings and all. He wrinkled his nose as the rough hands applied the runny liquid between his toes and hopped on one foot and then the other as his soles were bathed to complete the work. Without further ado, he was marched back into the great chamber and stood before the main fire pit.

There, a member of the elders' circle rose and wrapped a warrior's apron around David's waist, a bright yellow weave decorated with artful seals. Then he was given necklaces, and bands of woven shells were put around his wrists and ankles, each one accompanied by a long story about its significance, words unfortunately lost on the frightened boy. He was crowned with a downy head-dress and his shoulders sagged under the weight of a heavy robe of ermine, glistening white with rich black markings running down its length.

The drums now grew more powerful and a massive bundle of seaweed was dropped onto the fire, causing the flames to give way to a mushroom of white smoke. David was instantly whisked away and led up a ladder to a high platform above the dirt floor. The seaweed was drowned by a bucket of salt water and the blanket of smoke cleared away as if by magic.

The crowd was left buzzing, startled by the sudden disappearance of their honoured guest, but their attention was drawn to a line of painted warriors holding torches high over their heads. All eyes followed the flickering light until it brightened enough to reveal the Spirit Child standing in his magnificent clothes high above them, his arms outstretched to greet them. They broke out in song once more, shouting and singing. They danced the raven dance, the deer dance, and one skilful warrior donned a bear skin and, holding his hand over one eye, danced the story of the great bear David had managed to elude that very morning. The frog dance followed, and finally the dance of the thunderbird, most important of all the deities.

From high above, the English boy sat on a soft, fur-covered throne watching them. He was as bewildered and as frightened as ever, still ignorant of the meaning of this wild celebration. He waved politely when a villager cried out to him, but he prayed silently for rescue. His prayer, however, was interrupted by a young warrior who crept up to him and laid a bowl of raspberries at his feet. Another appeared carrying a tray of cooked seafoods and a third with clear water and the juice from mashed blackberries. He dipped his fingers again and again into the delicious berry pastes, licking each finger separately to savour the sweetness. For the first time since his arrival, he felt stuffed, and gradually he relaxed, knowing that he was, at least for now, not about to die.

Night swept over the village, taking the exhausted boy into a fitful sleep. The drums beat on and he felt his body circling in the air, his head swimming and his stomach swollen with delicious food. When he came to, he found that everyone was too busy to notice him, and decided to risk trying to go outside. No one stopped him, and once he was through the door he breathed in the cool air and took his head-dress off to run his fingers through his sweat-soaked hair. As he stood quietly on the grassy knoll overlooking the moonlit beach, his thoughts turned to his father and the *Langley*. Here he was, free, no one watching him. He could throw off his heavy fur robe and all his trappings, and simply wade into the black water. They would never know . . .

"But if I run away, they'll become angry all over again," he said to himself. "And besides, they know these waters better than I do. If they like me, and if I do what they want, they might take me back to the ship if I ask them."

He would wait until morning at least and then, if their mood was as friendly — even admiring — as it seemed to be now, he would request a canoe and paddlers for a journey down the inlet. Having made up his mind, he turned back towards the celebrations in the longhouse, its loose planks spilling light from three fires into the night air. After one last

long breath, he entered and climbed the rickety ladder to his
throne above the crowded room.

Once he was seated, the shaman urged a frightened young
man towards him, one of the five or six natives David had
thought might be servants or slaves. The poor fellow knelt
before him, and one end of a fibre cord that led to a collar
around his neck was placed into the hand of the Spirit Boy.
David reached out and tapped the old priest on the shoulder,
attempting to hand the cord back to him, but the shaman
waved him off. As he did so, David caught sight of Nootka,
and an idea struck him immediately. If he was to have a
slave of some kind, he would choose her. She would be good
company, and she would no longer be roughly treated by the
old woman.

"Her!" he said to the shaman, pointing to the girl at the
same time.

The wizened old man nodded, took the cord and called
down to the slave girl. She came forward nervously and, after
climbing the ladder behind the platform, sat down at David's
feet. The crowd cheered once more and the music began all
over again, even louder than before. David was encouraged
by this last piece of good fortune. He had asked for something
he wanted and it had been given to him without hesitation.
He felt now that returning to the *Langley* might not be such a
difficult matter, once he was better understood.

Another wave of sleep almost overcame him, but it was
broken by the unmistakable shout of the chief, Tuklit. He
bellowed until the longhouse was still, and then he stepped
closer to the fire pit.

"I, Tuklit, will honour the Spirit Boy with a potlatch!" he
began. "It will be the greatest of all gift-giving ceremonies. I
will welcome people from every village to see the gift from
the gods. Everyone will see his magic and they will know

that Tuklit has been chosen by the gods to be the greatest chief of all!"

His words were not finished before the cheering began. Everyone leaped and danced, making the young captive wonder what the chief had said that was so exciting. He looked carefully from one side of the room to the other, watching the frogs dance and the deer dance, this time everyone dancing at once, so close to each other that there would be no room to fall if one of them tripped. Little did he realize what Tuklit was planning. The chief foresaw that David would, in a matter of a few short weeks, be the centre of a contest among a dozen villages to see which one could give him the most valuable gifts. He would be the richest and most honoured boy the coast would ever know for time to come, lavished with canoes and weapons, furs and fine carvings. Warm woven blankets would be his, and possibly a dozen more slaves would serve his needs. At the same time, Tuklit would become known as the chief whom the gods honoured, more important than even the great Maquinna, the wise leader of the Nootka peoples.

Even if he had known what they were, David was now beyond caring about potlatches. He had fallen asleep at last, his robed legs stretched out in front of him, his head bent to one side. The villagers, however, took his look of contented ease as a sign of his forgiveness and danced on into the night.

Fifteen

*E*ach day seemed longer aboard the *Langley*. Each empty hour brought greater sorrow to the crewmen and their officers as the longboats returned empty, without so much as a single clue to David's whereabouts. Occasionally, a longboat crew would sight an object floating on the water and all hands would lay on the oars until they were alongside a piece of woven reed matting or a broken native fishing net. The men would stare at the relic in disappointment and then move on in silence.

Every man feared the word that would soon have to be passed along, the word that the captain had given up hope and the search must end. As the days turned into weeks the crew came to expect it, and it became a burden on men's minds. What if they sailed from the inlet and left the boy alive out in the wilds waiting for someone to help him? What if a longboat were to turn one more rocky corner to see the boy waving from shore? Stranger things were known to have happened.

One late afternoon, a cutter piloted by Wiggins drew alongside the *Langley* and all hands rushed to the railing to see one of their mates hold up a shirt, torn and buttonless, that had once belonged to Link. The area immediately along the shore had been combed by the six men but it had turned up nothing more, not a footprint or a bent twig. This did not deter the ship's company, for four crews started at dawn the next day to walk the bush and rocky outcroppings, a foot search that took the men three miles up a narrow canyon. But this one small glimmer of hope sputtered and died, sending the men further into despair. The time had come to think about moving on to Nootka Sound, then home to England. That moment was the turn of the tide one cool grey morning.

"The current is ebbing now, Mr Perkins. Ready the sail and have the boats man the towline," Captain Spencer said quietly.

"Aye aye, Captain!"

The captain stood at the helm beside his first officer, his eyes rigidly set on the inlet water. No one dared look at him or test his temper. After five exhausting weeks of futile waiting, he had steeled himself to the truth and now did what he had to do — his duty to the King. Within minutes, the four cutters were busy swinging the vessel around, gradually lining up her bow with the narrow channel through the granite ramparts. The ebb tide gradually picked up the heavy round hull and the *Langley* began to drift forward on her own. A shout went up and the longboats were brought to her side and hauled aboard.

Grimsbey eyed the captain from a position off the starboard rail and, when the crewmen were busy aloft, he walked slowly up the steep gangway to the helm.

"Excuse me, sir."

"Huh? Oh yes, bosun. What do you want?"

Grimsbey removed his wrinkled cap from his balding head. "I . . . I would make me offer again, sir, if it would please you. I be good and willing to remain here to continue the search while you take the ship to Nootka and back. All I need is three good tars, Bixby and Peters among 'em."

The captain did not answer immediately. After a while he bowed his head and without further delay spoke in a low voice.

"Your generosity has been noted and appreciated, bosun. However, my man, we are under orders from the highest authority to make for Nootka Sound and then come about for England. Therefore we should not return here to pick you up." He swallowed hard and gazed out on the water. "Anyhow, Grimsbey, the ship requires all hands in case of foul weather. Agreed?"

"Aye aye, Captain. As you say, sir."

"Full sail, Mr Perkins. All working canvas!"

"Full sail it is, sir," Perkins answered over a large lump in his throat.

Somewhere behind them in the mysterious inlet lay four secrets — the fates of Walters, Link, Havlock and the young Spencer. Were all of them marooned together on some jagged rock high in the channel? Or were they victims of some tribal rite? Perhaps they had been attacked by the carnivorous beasts that were said to lurk in the black forests. Last of all, they might be lying on some sandy beach, having drowned in the waters of the walled basin.

Every officer and man aboard had racked his brain to arrive at an answer to each of these grim questions. Each one vied for the privilege of finding the boy, the senior men knowing full well how handsome such a report would appear on their log, and each sailor privately believing that a large reward would be in the offing. None were sure just how much energy they should give to finding the whereabouts of the three tars, none save Mr Perkins. His head still wore the bruising reminder of his last dealings with them, and he would have liked to have seen them before the ship's court.

The *Langley*, now empty of spirit, pushed doggedly into the ocean swells and tacked northward on the last leg of her outward journey.

Sixteen

*D*avid Spencer, Spirit Child of the coastal nations, stretched out on his back on a gently rolling log in the middle of the inlet. He was surrounded by native brothers and sisters, all good friends, all helping him to enjoy his topsy-turvy world. For weeks he had been safe, free from the taunts and bruises that had greeted him during his first two days in the village.

Each day began when he climbed down from his high shelf in the shaman's lodge, fresh from a long sleep between soft bear and mink rugs. He usually wakened two friends in an adjoining family chamber and ran down the brisk cold pebbles of the beach for an early morning swim. Breakfast, eaten on the sunny beach, included every kind of wild fresh fruit found in the deep forest. Sometimes a seagull egg was added, fried to a tender crisp on a white hot rock from the fire pit, an idea David had introduced. Often the boys would join a fishing party sailing down the inlet towards the far beaches. David was keenly aware that somewhere along these forbidding walls was an opening that would eventually lead him back to his ship, and he carefully studied every point and small bay. Certainly he had realized, after several short hikes into the back hills, that there was no way out by footpath: every well-worn trail ended abruptly at the face of a tall cliff.

Sometimes the youths would load a small piece of drift-wood with tiny stones and fix a thin mast to its middle. Then they would push it out on the tide and throw rocks at it until its narrow deck was cleared or until the wood escaped their reach. When they tired, they would sit on the granite rocks and carve small canoes from cedar strips, cutting tiny designs into the hulls to match those of their fathers' skilful handiwork. These frail craft would be pushed along the shallows, sometimes coming to a fateful end in a mock battle.

Most of the warm days were spent in the water, David always accompanied by his seal pup. This partnership was a vital one, although he did not realize it, for it strengthened his magic power in the eyes of the native boys, ensuring his safety in the village. On very hot days they would swim two or three miles out into the inlet without a rest or climb up on some giant boulder and dive down to the soft sandy bottom to test the wily, foot-wide crabs, fighting them with bare hands. Once caught, the beasts would be raised to the surface and dropped into a waiting canoe for a short journey home to the cooking bowl.

Lunch was not a separate meal, for the children nibbled berries and bits of venison and dried cod throughout the day whenever they were hungry. In this way, they were always pleasantly full without ever having to stop their play to come into the longhouses to eat. Log-fighting was a special game that took hours out of any warm afternoon. A massive sea-worn tree trunk, smooth and sliverless, was eased out into the water from the beach and ten or twelve boys would climb onto it and begin to toss each other off into the salt brine. The last one left high and dry would be the chief — until he too was pushed off. This led to races on smaller timber, each contestant lying out flat on his log, legs over the sides to balance him, arms flailing the water into wild foam as he worked his way past lesser paddlers. The races always ended in loud but harmless arguments about who was the victor. More serious wrestling took place on the beach, usually when there were village girls to show off to, but even if they finished in anger, the fighters soon became friends once more.

David enjoyed "school" very much, those brief moments when the boys were taught how to spear a fleeing weasel or down a wild rabbit with bow and arrow. Fish traps were something the English boy avoided handling, the memory of his capture still too fresh. The lessons also helped him pick up new words, and after a while he was able at least to communicate simple thoughts and feelings.

After an early feast just before sunset, the younger boys and girls would follow their older brothers and sisters to the high cliffs opposite the village bay in their narrow canoes. There they would watch the bravest of the youths scale the cliffside and jump down into the inlet, falling sometimes fifty or sixty feet. When night fell, the most daring would hold pitch torches above their heads during their leaps, the flames glowing brilliantly in the rushing air and then dying in a sizzling cloud of steam as the bearers struck the water.

David's first experience out at the cliffs was one that Klutu would like to have forgotten. The native youth challenged the Spirit Boy to jump from a towering ledge, but once David reached the rocky outcropping and peered down, he found that it was not nearly as high as his leap from the *Langley*'s boom. He grinned and climbed up another thirty feet, leaving Klutu on the lower level to watch in amazement. Down he flew, striking the water with a tremendous splash, then bobbing up and waving to his friends along the rocks. The young villagers cheered and gathered around him, and when Klutu climbed down to them he too, albeit grudgingly, joined in the shouts of praise.

It was always exciting to join the older youths, though it was not always possible, for the native teenagers spent many long hours working alongside the adults, learning the crafts they would someday require to survive on the coastline. Some of the youths accompanied the elders on long fishing expeditions which took them two or three hundred miles away. Others worked the adze and bone tools as they helped to fashion beautiful totem poles or massive cooking bowls from rich red cedar logs. A few boys worked with bone and animal claws under the stern hands of their fathers or uncles, filing and cutting the hard white materials until intricate pieces fit together to form a fish trap or a small ornament for a festival. Still others wandered through the dense brush on the mountain ridges, hunting for young deer or game birds.

Their sisters, who kept a bit apart from the boys, were just as busy throughout the long days learning to weave the beautiful baskets and clothing which David had collected on his longhouse shelf. They dyed the separate strands deep black and brown, interlacing these with the sun-dried yellow grasses, their fingers flying as they turned the slowly forming objects in their laps. Always at their feet lay the small babies who slept while their mothers cooked fish stews or picked fresh berries at the foot of the mountain.

The English boy looked forward to the evenings too because they always seemed to be times for feasting and celebration. Everything that happened in the village was celebrated — a new totem pole raised or a new canoe launched, a baby born or a young couple married, a successful hunt or a brush with death at the hands of a natural enemy. Every occasion had its own story and, always, its special dance.

The past few weeks had been extremely happy ones for the villagers because they had been blessed with the coming of the Spirit Child, and that was reason enough for them to regularly don their finest robes and dance until the grey sky heralded a new day. Often, the honoured one would fall asleep long before the night was over, but he would always wake up the following mornings deep in his fur bedding.

David could not help comparing his life here in the village with his sometimes unhappy, tedious hours on the *Langley*. How was he to long for the ship and its hours of hard, grueling labour when his days here were filled with swimming, games and laughter? How could he make himself miss the salted, year-old beef and stale mouldy bread as he sat gorging himself with savoury venison and soft sweet strawberries, the tangy liquid sliding down his tongue? And, apart from Grimsbey and perhaps Peters, who would he miss aboard the lonely vessel? Here he had at least thirty good friends — even Klutu left him alone to go his own way. No, he had to admit, he was not in a great hurry to get back to the anchorage, even if his father was waiting for him. With the exceptions of Tuklit and Klutu, the life and the people here were good.

Perhaps tomorrow he would paddle back to the ship, or maybe the day after, he thought as he lay on his favourite log out on the water under the hot sun. Three friends sat near him, warming their backs in the hot rays while they lazily picked at the soft bark beneath their toes. The seal pup swam in circles around Nootka as she clung to the end of the water-logged timber beside another native girl.

Suddenly the peaceful calm was shattered by the cry of a boy on the far beach. "Potlatch! Potlatch! They are coming!" he cried over and over again.

Seventeen

*T*he signal "potlatch" was enough to send the native children swimming ashore at full clip, arms and legs thrashing the cool water as fast as they could. David and his pup swam among them, still totally mystified, and then he flipped over onto his back to see what was creating such a stir. There they were, barely visible in the harsh glare — a half-dozen large canoes in a close-knit group, sailing very low in the water, all heading for the shore. Instantly he increased his strokes until his feet touched the sandy bottom. Raising his hand, he sent the seal pup back out into the bay and clambered out over the smooth pebbles.

The grass bluff was crowded with villagers, all running in different directions, some daubing paint on their glistening skins, others toting baskets of food and furs from one place to another. Tuklit shouted orders, waving his arms about, stamping his feet at the same time, adding to the already fever-pitched excitement. The aged shaman saw David wandering through the mad throng and grasped his arm, speaking to him in solemn tones. He led the confused boy into his longhouse where the old women waited with his robes and decorations and the ever-present stone dish of smelly oil. He had grown accustomed to being greased from head to toe with the slippery liquid and he stood perfectly still, his hands firmly clutching the belt of his ragged leggings. Within minutes he was once more decked out in his finery, his white ermine robe gleaming in the sun's rays which streaked through the rooftop. His shell necklace had been polished and his hat refurbished with fresh down from a swan. Just the sight of him awed his new friends all over again, and even Nootka kept her distance.

He was led solemnly outdoors and hidden behind the platform erected especially for the potlatch. He stood under the centre of the shaky boards and peeked out over the inlet. His jaw fell open as he drank in the spectacle of thirty war canoes, splendid craft, decorated from bow to stern with fresh, brilliant dyes, each vessel topped by a massive prow supporting a long-necked wooden bird or animal figure. Behind the magnificent carvings, small stages were fashioned, each platform graced by a strangely draped dancing figure, arms waving in the air. As the craft edged towards the beach, they manoeuvred into a formation that stretched from one side of the bay to the other, a spell-binding sight that riveted every eye upon it. The villagers broke out of their trance into a resounding cheer and the volley was answered by an equally vibrant chorus from the newcomers, all of whom stood on their feet without so much as teetering one canoe.

David's eyes widened as he watched the gifts being unloaded and carried up onto the beach. Arms were weighted down with folds of reed mats, conical hats and seasoned furs. Shell beads and whale tooth necklaces reflected the sunlight, and polished carvings in red and tanned woods added to the array of colour. The boy was especially interested in a twenty-foot-long canoe being carefully set down at the water's edge, and he longed to try it in the inlet to see how fast it would cut through the mirrored surface. Little did he realize that all of these beautiful presents were his.

Far out in the inlet itself, a speck could be seen, at least a mile distant, a latecomer struggling against the changing tide. A plump, red-faced chief squatted on his undersized platform at the bow and his son, an equally plump young boy about David's age, sat in a ball at his feet, a small spear tight in his fat fist.

Suddenly the chief grunted as he pointed to a small silver head swimming alongside the sluggish craft, its curious eyes darting back and forth. At the urging of his father, the boy climbed to his feet, balanced himself on the rough planks and then raised his spear. The father roared a command at the reluctant hunter and when the boy hesitated, he plucked the spear from his hand and thrust it downward. It struck the little animal, causing it to lurch and then roll deeper into the dark water. The spear broke free and floated to the surface, its tip surrounded by a small pool of blood. The proud chieftain tossed his head back and pushed out his chest, shouting to his paddlers at the same time. Finally, this last canoe lumbered into the shore and its cargo was set down on the beach.

Tuklit swept down the well-worn path in his ceremonial robe and bellowed a welcome to the newcomers. David watched him as he bowed and flung his arms out to receive the heavy basket filled with handsome gifts. Once he had led the weary party to the grass bluff above the beach, he called for silence and then mounted the wooden stage.

"Friends of the potlatch, hear me! I am Tuklit, the chief whom the gods have chosen to bless! I have served the gods well as a great chief and I have been rewarded. Now I wish to share my good fortune with you all."

A thunderous cheer rose over the village, not so much for Tuklit as for the mountain of gifts stacked high against the longhouse beside him.

"Now it is time for my shaman to bring you my gift from the gods. Bring the Spirit Child, Shaman!"

The crowd milled closer, some pushing and shoving immediately below the wooden platform. Warriors hoisted their spears upward as the old shaman climbed the steps followed by the Spirit Child, resplendent in his fine regalia. A gasp could be heard as the boy was gently prodded to the front of the platform, and small children pressed forward to see this mysterious gift-person. A few muffled voices in the back of the throng could be heard exchanging words, some of them in angry tones.

"We have seen a pale warrior before!" one bold man shouted.

"So have we, so have we," more joined in.

"Wait — just wait, I say," Tuklit shouted in return. "Hear my words. Yes, he is a white warrior's boy. You have seen some bigger than this one, but you have not heard the child speak to the animals. You have not heard the animals answer him. The gods have given him powers. I say to you, he *is* a Spirit Child!"

The chief's booming voice floated out over the crowd and hushed the protesters in their tracks. No one dared to follow with so much as a whisper after such an outburst. The huge man's voice was easily matched by his rippling, muscular body, which strained under his long reed robe.

Once the chief had restored order, he swung around and pointed to the beach. "Come, all of you here. The Spirit Child will cast his magic for you now. Follow me to the waters of the bay."

With that, he stepped down off the flimsy boards and began his slow proud march to the water's edge. The shaman was next in line, David beside him. The old man whispered to the boy in his strange tongue, evidently offering him words of encouragement. David was not the least bit comforted, however, for he had no clear idea what was happening, nor what his future held. The word "potlatch" meant nothing to him, nor did the gifts and visiting villagers fill him any longer with delight. He looked around for some kind of reassurance, but found none. Everyone's face was solemn, every pair of lips sealed, even Nootka's as she followed at his heels. He took slow, careful steps down the grassy bank, stretching out the time as best he was able. A long look out into the inlet gave him no heart, and a quick glance behind him at the two hundred or more natives did nothing for his spirits except drive them even lower.

The expectant crowd closed on the beach, gathering in a wide arc at the shoreline, leaving room for the chief, the shaman, the Spirit Child and Nootka to find their way into the shallows. The old man leaned towards the boy and pointed to the sand below his feet. He grunted and moved his hand in a wide circle. David's heart immediately lightened as he guessed what they wanted him to do. "The seal pup again," he whispered to himself. "They want me to do more tricks with him."

He took a long breath in relief, a great weight lifted off his shoulders. Quickly he slipped out of his ermine robe and handed it to Nootka. Then he unfastened his necklaces and removed his head-dress of down and passed them to the shaman as he turned to face the inlet. He waded slowly into the refreshing water and stopped when he was knee-deep. He scanned the calm surface and raised his head. "Arf...arf! Come on — come on, little seal!"

He waited. The water remained glassy calm under the sun's rays.

"Come on, boy!" he called. "Come on, little seal."

Nothing. The crowd remained silent.

"Here, little seal, here seal!" he pleaded.

He waded deeper into the water. After another series of calls, he dove under and with wide eyes searched the murky green world around him. He popped up to the surface to call once more as he treaded water. Each time his voice floated across the inlet, a small, wounded seal raised its head very weakly and tried to answer. But all it could manage was a weak, noiseless sigh.

The visitors were growing restless and, after David had almost lost his voice from wear, they began to speak out and then shout, demanding to see some kind of magic to answer for their long travels and splendid gifts. "Is this the best you can show us? You, the greatest of all chiefs?"

Certainly Tuklit was losing his patience. He whispered angrily to the shaman, threatening the old man, causing him to wade out into the water to stand beside the frightened boy. The shaman placed his hand on David's shoulder and talked to him in his own quiet gentle way. The boy understood what he wanted but as hard as he tried, he could not coax his pup into shore. His throat tightened in panic and he was unable to utter a sound. His tongue was dry, almost stuck tight to the roof of his mouth, and beads of sweat ran down his neck under his ears. "What happened to my pup?" he wondered. "Oh please...come and help me, little seal." He held his hand to his forehead to shield his eyes from the reflection off the water and tried to swallow over his raspy tongue.

The visitors were no longer able to contain their anger. Tuklit had tried to fool them, bringing them here laden with valuable presents. He had been known to plan potlatches before, and then fail to prepare his own village's gifts in time for the exchanging ceremony. His talk was as big as the mountain that stood behind his village, his stories as tall as the cedars standing on the clifftops, but his actions were those of a chipmunk — noisy, but very small. And now the crowd pressed closer to the shoreline, goading the huge man with insults, threatening him, daring him to bring forth his sign from the gods. They pushed forward, forcing some of their number deeper and deeper into the warm tide. When David glanced quickly at the pressing mob, he shuddered at the fierce anger that lit their faces. Even some of his own villagers were joining in with them, growing more impatient with him, minute by frightening minute.

Once more he gazed out into the inlet. There was no sign of the seal pup. Now, at the centre of this great throng, he was truly alone.

Eighteen

*T*hree ships lay at anchor in Nootka Sound. They were the *Langley*, the American *Liberty* and the Spanish *El Marcos*. The trio was surrounded by fleets of friendly canoes and white longboats, sailors and Indians bartering for what were treasures in each man's eyes — furs and reed hats for one, shiny glass beads for the other. The rain had not begun to fall, but low clouds threatened throughout the morning.

Perkins, Wiggins and young Scarfe plied between the Spaniard and Yankee ships, paying their respects in keeping with good custom, while the doctor found himself at the feet of the great Maquinna, the giant, awesome chief of the Nootka, a man to be feared. The leader sat in splendour, surrounded by possibly seventy slaves, the doctor estimated, and another twenty Nootka warriors, each one attending to his every command. A young native sat nearby, translating what English words he knew into the dialect of the region. The Englishman hoped that what Maquinna was finally hearing was satisfactory to him. This was no time for a misunderstanding.

Captain Spencer remained on board in his cabin, a prisoner of his own making, ill with grief and unable to fully perform his duties. He had eaten little of late and was seldom seen beyond the massive oak door. One of the skeleton crew left on board, Glennesk, the ship's carpenter, stepped down the aft hatch and descended the narrow staircase. He knocked and awaited a reply.

"Who is it?"

"The carpenter, sir."

"What do you want, Glennesk?"

"I would have a word with you, Captain."

A long, uncomfortable moment of silence followed. "Well, come in."

The dwarf-like fellow slid around the door and drew himself up to the chart table. "Begging your pardon, sir, but I've this here carving for you."

Captain Spencer swung slowly around, his haggard, unshaven face showing no sign of interest. "Oh? Well put it on the table then."

The carpenter set a three-foot-high cross on the table, a beautifully carved piece, intricate shells and leaves raised on its highly polished surface. Captain Spencer eyed it for a long time, then nodded and spoke in a hushed voice.

"It is a fine piece of work, Glennesk. I — I compliment you. Let me see it here. Ah, yes. . ."

The captain reached out and handed the cross back to the carpenter, but the poor man threw up his hands. "Oh, no, sir. I want you — that is, we wants you to have it, sir. The crew and me, we figured you might be wanting to set it on the beach when we gets back to the inlet, sir."

"Well, that is most noble, carpenter, but we must make way directly to the Sandwich Islands once we are done with our business here. I am sorry."

"Oh...Aye, aye. Sandwiches, sir. Aye," the carpenter nodded, barely hiding his disappointment. "Well, best you keeps this carving just the same, sir. It'll do the men better, if you know what I mean, if you'll pardon me, sir."

"Yes, I suppose so."

"I'll just leave it, then?" Glennesk asked.

"Very well, my man."

"I, ah, I best be getting back to me duties," the little man said nervously.

"Huh? Oh, yes, fine. Right you are," Spencer replied absentmindedly.

Once the carpenter had drawn the door closed, Captain Spencer rose and placed the carving on the chart table. He carefully unrolled a recent work over the cross and ran his finger down the outline of the coast, stopping at the ill-fated inlet. For the hundredth time he heard the small voice echo through the dimly lit chamber: "Please, sir, I want to go with you..."

After a long, tense moment of reflection on what might have been, he returned to his chair and resigned himself to brooding through another day. He wasn't sure how much time passed before the doctor knocked on the door and entered the stuffy cabin without waiting to be invited. Biggs sat himself down on a hard bench and heaved a sigh as he slipped off his heavy boots. He remained silent for a short period waiting for Captain Spencer to open a conversation.

"How is Chief Maquinna?" the captain asked finally.

"He is certainly fit, I can say that much for him. He is the single most powerful chieftain on this coast, I imagine. Has nerves of steel and a brain to match any. He pretty well decides what happens here and who will make it happen, I expect. He is also, I think, a bit miffed that you are ignoring him. He says that you should come ashore and feast with him regardless. His own shaman lost a granddaughter some months ago, possibly near the same inlet, while the child's father was fishing. She wandered off too. I think Maquinna understands your feelings somewhat. He wanted me to tell you how sorry he was."

"Kind of him."

The doctor fiddled with his pipe. "Ah... will you go ashore?"

"I must remain here aboard ship, Doctor. You have my permission to go along and extend my thanks to the chief," Captain Spencer replied solemnly, and then his attention turned to a strange-looking bone and cord contraption lying on the low table next to his chair. "What is this?"

"Fish trap of some kind, I believe. These two bony hooks slip over the back of a salmon and, as he swims away, they tighten, sinking into his flesh. He tried to explain how it was made but I'm afraid I lost the drift half-way through his directions."

"Quite clever, by the look of them."

The doctor managed to light his pipe on the fourth try. He drew a deep puff and sat back against an oak panel. "The chief tells me he was invited to a potlatch but waited here to greet you instead."

"You say a potlatch? I've always wanted to see one — chiefs from different clans exchanging gifts, trying to outdo each other. If they are worth their salt, they are supposed to hold them once a year. Shame Maquinna missed it."

"Apparently he wasn't upset. Claims the fellow in charge of

this one was a bit of a — oh, how did the translator put it?
— a show-off, I think. Always giving potlatches, this time for
a Spirit Child!"

"Spirit Child?" the captain looked up as he spoke.

"Yes, apparently sent along by the gods. I say, what's this?"
the doctor interrupted himself as he reached over to lift the
wooden cross from the chart table.

"The ship's carpenter presented it to me. It was his plan, and
that of the crew, to set it up on the shore where Davie was last
thought to have been. . ." Captain Spencer turned away. "I
thought it was awfully decent of them, but I had to confess to
Glennesk that we were returning to the Sandwich Islands and
on to England directly."

"Pity," the doctor said as he turned the carving over and set
it back down on the table.

Nineteen

*D*avid attempted one more desperate call for his seal pup with a husky, spent voice, but it was no use. Even if the little animal was close by, the boy thought, he probably couldn't hear over the angry howls of the onlookers. Men, women and children from a dozen villages shouted at the tops of their lungs, aiming their sharp tongues at Tuklit. At the same time, the visitors were being urged to take to their canoes by their equally angry — and embarrassed — hosts.

"Silence!" Tuklit repeated as he climbed up onto his lofty platform. "Listen to me. We will feast and then the Spirit Child will show you his magic. He is not ready."

More howls of protest erupted, peppered with name-calling and insults, some meant for the chief, others hurled in the opposite direction towards the small stricken boy standing in the shallows. The old shaman moved in front of David and held out his cloak to shield the terrified victim from the bombardment.

"Shaman!" Tuklit cried, as he ducked out of the way of a spinning stick, "Do something. Beat the boy. Make him show his magic!"

David could not understand the words flying around him, but he knew too well that he was responsible for this frenzied outburst from the mob. He wanted to run and hide somewhere, but there was nowhere to go. He stood helplessly as the guests swarmed down the beach to their dugouts. His eye caught sight of still more visitors pouring in and out of the longhouses, laden with their own gifts and as many other treasures as they could carry. The villagers chased after them with branches and pieces of driftwood, beating their backs as they closed in on them. Soon spears were flying over canoes drawing hastily away from the shore, and dozens of youths waded chest-deep just to fling one last rock at the fleeing parties. In a few calamitous moments the beach was deserted except for the gaunt, bent shaman, the broken-hearted chief, a forlorn, lost boy and a small Nootka girl huddled at his feet.

The fuming Tuklit shifted from one foot to the other, fire flickering in his eyes. First he glared down at David and then at the shaman.

"Move, old man," he growled. "Give me the boy."

"No, I will not, Tuklit. It is my duty to protect the Spirit Child."

"You do not dare tell me, Tuklit, what your duty is, Shaman. Your duty is to me!" the chief stormed, stepping closer to David and the brave old man.

"Do not touch one hair on this boy's head," the shaman warned him.

"Why you, you dare to — Move! Move out of the way!"

"I will not move," the shaman answered defiantly, staring directly into Tuklit's burning eyes.

The confused, shaken villagers had gathered on the bluff

above the beach after the last of the canoes had shot out into the inlet, and now they stood silently as they followed the heated words between chief and shaman. As they watched, the talk ceased and the two adversaries faced each other, tight-lipped, eyes glaring, faces taut. David huddled behind the old man, Nootka squatting beside him, both holding their breaths in fear. The chief raised his powerful arm and shoved the shaman to one side with a mighty thrust, causing the ancient, spindly legs to fold. The shaman fell to the stones in a heap of tangled fur and brown, withered limbs. He tried desperately to climb to his feet but fell back again to lie on his side in great pain.

Now David and the girl stood alone before the crazed Tuklit, both shaking like gull feathers in the sea wind, both waiting for the next blow. Nootka crouched low, hiding her face in her apron, too frightened to watch. Tuklit hesitated, still expecting his shaman to regain his legs, but his eyes drifted from the stricken man to gaze around at the villagers standing behind him.

He became fidgety, angered that this moment of power should turn out to be so uncomfortable for him. He glanced again at the people on the bluff, then at David, and slowly drew his knife from his cloak and ran his fingers across the savage blade as he stepped towards the English boy. David stood up quickly and faced the enraged man, staring into his eyes, unblinking, stern, just as Grimsbey had said he should do when faced with a bully. The seconds ticked by — five . . . ten . . . twenty. . . . Tuklit was frozen in his tracks, afraid to move and afraid not to move . . .

"Go on, great Chief Tuklit!" a voice sang out. "Kill him! He can't fight back — you are safe!"

"What stops you, Tuklit? Are you afraid of the boy? How do you know he is not the Spirit Boy?" the older warriors scorned him. "You do not run from a weak old man. Face the boy!"

The furious chieftain could take no more. He flew around and, with head bowed low, stormed through the circle of villagers and hurried angrily to his longhouse, leaving two children and a gravely injured old priest on the shore to fend for each other.

David knelt at the shaman's side and tried to brush the bloodied hair from his forehead. The stricken man attempted to sit upright but settled back instead and opened his eyes. Reaching out, he grasped the boy's hand with his withered fingers.

"Tsakl-shgt-ligt. . ." he whispered.

"Taskl-shhh. . ." the boy tried to repeat.

"Nuklat-xathkut. . ."

Nootka took David by the arm and made a swimming motion. Then she pointed to the water and back to the old man.

"He must want me to swim away from here," the boy said aloud. "How am I supposed to do that, I wonder?"

As he spoke, the kindly priest gave a deep sigh and shut his eyes. His head rolled gently to one side and his fingers broke their grasp on the boy's arm. Slowly, his hand dropped to the pebbles by David's knee. The boy's eyes filled with tears. He placed his hand on the shaman's still chest and gazed out over the long inlet. Nootka sat motionless, her face showing little else but deep fear. Neither one felt the press of people gathering around them.

A younger woman, the mother of the two boys whom David played with most often, put her arm about the shattered boy's shoulders and quietly drew him to his feet. She, too, like the others standing about, had a face streaked with tears, and she stumbled as she guided David towards the longhouse at the top of the bluff. Nootka followed them and six warriors plodded along behind, carrying the body of the old man on their shoulders. A scattering of elders and children trudged after them, picking their way carefully over the hard pebbles, trailing along in what was becoming a lengthy procession. The women began to wail, and the mournful sound drifted across the village like a cold blue mist.

Inside the largest of the longhouses at the centre of the bluff, Tuklit could hear the mournful lament as it seeped through the cracks in the rough boards. He could not escape the eerie sounds as he squatted by the low fire, Klutu and some of the younger warriors surrounding him. Together they sat, painfully silent, neither looking up nor speaking to one another. Tuklit was filled with his own doubts and fears. He had just slain the man best loved by almost all the villagers, and much worse, he had tried to harm the captive boy. Now the village was indeed torn into two camps, just as the shaman had warned him. Here he was, chieftain of a handful of young warriors, all eager for war, all tired of the peaceful ways of the old priest and most of them secretly glad that he was no more. Yet they were but infants, inexperienced in battle and short in patience. He knew he might not be able to control them; they might not be satisfied unless they were able to whet their appetites in war.

As he sat, he pondered how he could bring an answer to the single burning question before the village: was the white captive a Spirit Child or not? Then a thought sparked in his mind and he nodded to himself as he rose. Once on his feet, he turned to face his thirty or so followers.

"Ever since the pale boy came to our village we have had trouble. He has taken our shaman away with his power and has broken our people's spirits, sending them into two houses."

He paused to let this new idea penetrate. The braves

glanced at one another to see how the chief's words were being accepted. Tuklit warmed to his story.

"It is time for the Spirit Child to be returned to the gods and punished for his behaviour. Then our village will be great and our warriors victorious in their battles."

Twice Klutu wanted to speak out and twice he drew back, afraid that his father might descend upon him in anger. Finally his patience ran dry. He struggled to his cramped feet.

"But Father, the pale boy does talk to the seal! I have seen him many times and. . ."

"Silence!" Tuklit bristled.

"I too have swum with the Spirit Boy, and he commands the animal. . ." another teenager broke in.

"Very well, then leave my house and join the wailing women and the old men and babies. Is that what you want?" Tuklit cried. "Is that your choice, coward?"

He knew he must make his move now or lose his band of doubting braves. "I will put your Spirit Boy to the test. I will take him out to the whale god and ask the killer whale if he is a Spirit or not. If the killer whale spares him, then I will believe he is of the Spirits. Only then will I listen to the stories, for I am Tuklit, greatest of all the chiefs. I have spoken."

He raised his arms over his head and gazed into the glow above the fire pit. He began to sing a battle song, loud enough to drown out the mournful dirge floating across the compound. His young warriors rose as one and joined in with robust, throaty cries, their own arms raised high. After a few minutes of song, Tuklit waved his hands for silence.

"Go now out into the night and find the pale child. Bring him here to me and we will prepare him for the journey to the sea. He will have the slave girl as his companion in the deep waters. Let the whale god decide! Go, all of you. Down to the shore and bring the two to me at once."

Twenty

*T*he unexpected departure of His Majesty's Ship *Langley* was followed with concern by the American and Spanish vessels, dozens of weathered tars eyeing the forlorn British ship as she slowly made way towards the open water. Her full set of sail bagged little wind and her great flag hung limp above her stern. It was a quiet evening, a night in which a man could hear a voice across the water as if it were whispered into his very ear. The sea was deadly calm, the glassy surface reflecting a thin scattering of cloud hovering to the west.

Not more than an hour out of the Sound, the course was set for the Sandwich Islands, five thousand miles to the southwest. This point was ordered by Mr Perkins, who was now acting as ship's captain. It was not likely that Captain Spencer would appear on deck for some time. Perkins stood fast at the helm, the great spiked wheel in the hands of Grimsbey. Neither man spoke beyond the necessary "Steady" and "Steady she be, sir." There was no light-hearted banter, no talk of home and sweethearts, no tales of sea or ships.

Below the helm, seamen moved listlessly about, stowing gear and making sure that lines were secure. Nothing loose was to be tolerated, for even the gentlest of seas could clear a deck in one long roll. In the fo'c's'le a few hands leaned on the polished table under a low lamp, pondering the rumour that had worked its way around the ship, the talk about Maquinna's shaman and the weather. The old witch doctor had let it be known to one or another of the young officers that a terrible storm awaited any vessel that dared set sail before the week was out. He had warned that certain death was in the offing. However, the men knew well enough that no matter how grief-stricken he was, the captain would not suffer the likes of an old soothsayer to make up his mind for him. They accepted as one that Captain Spencer himself had given the order to sail. They had guessed wrong.

Perkins had taken the ship in hand after meeting with the doctor and the ship's officers. All had agreed that the captain was in no fit condition to be master of the *Langley* and that he had, weeks before, planned to leave for England once the flag had been shown in Nootka Sound. Any hope of a return to the ill-fated inlet was now fading, and the crew was settling down for a painful, empty journey home.

Grimsbey eyed the thin line of grey cloud on the horizon, wondering where it had come from since, only moments before, the sky had been clear save for a wisp of white in the west. He felt almost no breeze and the gulls above his head had to work to keep aloft. Perkins leaned an elbow on the port rail, absentmindedly watching the blue-green hills slip beyond the rim of the sea's arc.

"Taking the watch, sir," a voice broke the silence.

"Very well, sailor," Perkins replied. "Eight bells already? Grimsbey, read the course, if you will."

"Two hundred and twenty-two degrees, direct sou'-sou'west, sir."

"Two twenty-two, sir!" the younger seaman repeated.

"Carry on, man. Steady."

"Steady she be, sir."

Perkins turned to Grimsbey. "Oh, bosun?"

"Aye, sir?" Grimsbey stopped short.

"You know the captain better than any of us."

"That might well be, sir."

The officer moved closer so that he might not be overheard. "Ah, do you think he will come around? I mean, has he . . . has he ever behaved in this manner since you've known him?"

"He's had no need to be so sad afore, Mr Perkins. Losing the bairn means he's seen the end of the line, aye, the end of his family. Methinks the captain will be seaworthy not too long from now, aye."

"Yes. Of course you're right, bosun. Quite right! Thank you, my good fellow."

Perkins buttoned his jacket casually, for the wind had picked up and had swung around from the west to a more northerly direction. Soon the sails filled out into broad billows and picked up the ship at a much faster clip. Her bow dipped easily into the long Pacific swells and her masts took the increasing strain with ease. Perkins had forgotten about the cloud layer off to the west and now that darkness had erased any sign of it, the mate settled down to an uneventful long watch. He wished to double his duty so that the younger officers might gain some rest from their hours of toasting and eating aboard the visiting ships back in Nootka Sound.

Both the seaman and the first officer noticed the flash and glanced nervously at one another. The second bolt of lightning lit up the sky before the first roll of thunder barrelled over the ship. Another and yet another flash danced across the black sky, lighting up the sails in hideous blues, sparking out instantly, making the darkness richer than before. Gusts of wind swept over the helm and through the rigging, whistling a mournful song familiar to every jack-tar aboard. The vessel began to pitch to one side and then drop back again. Perkins bundled up and stood, feet astride, riding out the ship's unpredictable wallowing, wondering all the while whether he should report the storm to Captain Spencer.

Just then a monstrous ribbon of blue-white heat shot down from the heavens and ripped through the mainsail forward, the flames quickly blown out by the mounting winds. Ugly pieces of scorched canvas toppled down over the yards, floated to the deck and then into the angry sea. Perkins watched the sky for a second bolt and was greeted by an enormous crash of thunder.

A sheet of lightning painted an outline of Grimsbey as he mounted the top step of the helm and climbed towards Perkins. The *Langley* leaned at an awkward angle, hanging there for what seemed an endless second, but finally righted herself. Grimsbey hung on and then worked his way to the rain-soaked first officer.

"You be wanting all hands to stand to?" the bosun hollered over the wind.

"Not yet, Grimsbey!" Perkins shouted back.

"Methinks they best be put to service now, Mr Perkins!" Grimsbey bellowed through his waving beard.

"I am the officer in command, Mr Grimsbey."

"Aye, while we're still afloat, sir, if you'll forgive me, sir."

The ship dipped down into a deep trough, leaving the helm high in mid-air, the men clinging to whatever they might. Once the deck had levelled somewhat, Perkins fought his way over to Grimsbey and hung onto the rail as he leaned into his ear. "I, sir, am a man of thirty years and I have been at sea for eleven of those years, Mr Grimsbey. Hear me?" he demanded.

"Aye, sir. I hears ye!" Grimsbey shot back before he flung both arms about a compass guard. The ship leaned-to as a tremendous swell lifted her up like a cork and set her back again. "I meself have messed about on these here oceans for some fifty of me fifty-nine years, Mr Perkins. Now, I calls all hands, sir. Is that your order?"

Before Perkins could bark a reply, the stern of the ninety-foot vessel slipped backward into a long valley of black water and took a wave that almost caused her to flounder. The first officer was drenched to the skin with a mixture of salt spray and rain, as were the helmsman and Grimsbey. The frightened young officer was convinced now that the fifty years was the better of the two records at sea, and as he helplessly pressed the water down the front of his jacket with his one free hand, he nodded. "Very well. All hands, bosun."

Every man was concerned at the moment with saving his own skin as he fell on or hung onto anything that seemed secure. One by one the crewmen crawled along the companionways, dodging barrels of bully beef that had broken free and stepping over scattered belongings that washed up and down the inner decking with every sudden lurch and roll. Not a word was heard from the captain's quarters.

The helm was littered with black strips of canvas sail turned into slippery mush by the rain and sea. Grimsbey lashed himself to the wheel and Perkins held on nearby, counting the men as they emerged from the fo'c's'le, the sky alight with sheets of electricity. As each salt-soaked tar pulled himself free of the hatch, he craned his neck into the blinding rain to snatch a glimpse of the rigging. It was clear at once that no man would be ordered aloft, for there was little sail left to furl. All the main and forward canvas flapped in ghostly ribbons above their heads. The men clung to the lifelines strung about and to the sheets, some of the lines snapping with the pull of the yards. The sea heaved up on all sides and lapped across the deck like some monstrous dragon's tongue, spitting phosphorescent green fire from its hungry mouth. A scream was heard amid the howls of wind and quickly a huddle of bodies bent over an unconscious lad, holding him from being dashed against the rails or drowned in the driving rain.

"Tell them to cut the sheets, Mr Perkins!" Grimsbey cried out. "It ain't no use winding in the blighters!"

"I say, my man, that would. . ." Perkins began, but before he could finish, the *Langley* keeled over and lay on her starboard beam like a toy in a child's hands. Every man aboard was frozen with fear and waited breathlessly as she held and then slowly regained her stance as much as the sea would allow. Perkins sang out the order to slice through the remaining lines, knowing full well who was in charge now, and he was silently grateful that Grimsbey was at his side. The old bosun seemed almost to be enjoying himself, face high into the wind, beard flying and eyes twinkling in the momentary blue flashes.

A second mountainous wave struck the belaboured vessel full on her starboard beam and laid her so far off her centre that she was on the verge of capsizing. Instead, she toppled back upright but kept right on rolling over until she was once more in jeopardy. Grimsbey held fast to the wheel, tight-lipped and steady-eyed, showing not a flicker of fear. Perkins and the rest of the seamen, paralysed by fear, were unable to move. A brilliant sheet of lightning swept over the listing vessel as she fought for her life, and the eerie glow brought to light a gaunt, stiff figure. Captain Spencer was standing ghostlike by the compass, an arm firmly around the oak stanchion.

Once the *Langley* had found her ballast and heaved

upright, the captain released his grip and moved across to the helm.

"I believe the worst is over, Grimsbey," he said in a calm, firm manner.

"Aye," Grimsbey answered, showing no sign of surprise at finding his master on deck.

Perkins swung around in the blackness as a lesser swell picked up the ship. "Alright, Grimsbey, we can — Oh! Ah, sir, I didn't know..."

"Have the men secure all loose sheets once they are cut, Mr Perkins. You may go below and assist the doctor with any injured. Report damages to me when you have made a survey."

"Yes, sir!" the relieved Perkins replied.

"And have a good look about for signs of loose caulking. All seams, Mr Perkins!"

"Aye aye, sir!"

Each wave seemed less mountainous than the one before until the sea returned, at long last, to a reasonable temper. The *Langley* was not, however, back to normal, for sail left unscathed by the web of lightning had been torn to shreds by the onslaught of the near hurricane. The captain knew that once the morning light made work possible, all hands would have to set to pulling fresh canvas from the hold and stringing new sheets through the pulleys. The task now was to keep the drifting hull into the waves, trusting that her rudder would be a match for the difficult manoeuvre.

Within minutes, the word had carried from stem to stern, from scupper to scupper. The captain was in command and the ship safe. Somehow the two messages fit together, and all hearts beat with a fresh pulse.

Twenty-One

*T*he night wind carried the cries of the native women over the rooftops of the longhouses and out into the mist-covered inlet. They knelt beside the body of their shaman in the centre of the great cedar hall, their heads held high, their eyes closed, seeking a vision from the gods that would herald peace for their village. At the entrance, five warriors stood guard, expecting at any moment an attack by the younger men and youths who would be seeking the Spirit Child. Another ten armed men sat huddled to one side of the grim chamber surrounding the bewildered English boy and his Nootka friend. They spoke in low voices, scarcely heard under the high-pitched song of the mourners.

From where David squatted he could barely see the entrance, but he was sure that there was some disturbance taking place, for one man after another climbed out of the small outlet and back again, all the while facing the dark gap, spears poised to be thrown at a command. One of the natives ran back to the outchamber and huddled with the boy's guardians. In hurried words and rapid gestures, he seemed to be warning the listeners of some imminent danger. Immediately, all the men rose and moved off to another area, leaving the boy to himself.

After some time it was decided that David was not safe in the longhouse. Tuklit's young braves had just been turned away with the idea that no one knew where the lad was, but they were sure to return to the shaman's lodge, demanding to search the building from roof to floor. There would likely be blood shed before the hunt was over. Quickly the Spirit Child was escorted to the rear of the great chamber and provided with a reed pouch full of venison pieces and dried salmon. His two closest native friends appeared out of the darkness and were also provided with small packets of food. The native boys listened with rapt attention as they were instructed to seek out a hiding place unknown to any warrior and stay until a signal of many drums was sent up to them on the wind. The boys, it was felt, would have no trouble finding a place that would be impossible for others to find. Without so much as a creak of a board, long planks at the rear wall were pried loose and the three refugees gently prodded between them into the inky blackness.

They crept cat-like through the scrub brush, deftly picking their way along the damp trail until their eyes became accustomed to the shadows. Then they walked more confidently, silently, not even breathing heavily for fear of being overheard. The wind whistled through the treetops two hundred feet above their heads and sometimes two massive, swaying trunks scraped against one another, giving off a plaintive sound. They dared not snap a twig or lose their footing as they began to climb the granite wall at the base of the mountain. Every so often they stopped to listen for the footsteps of pursuers, then continued on upward, never looking below them lest they lose their nerve. Suddenly a streak of silver lightning flashed above the trees and the two village boys cringed in fear, stopping in their tracks so abruptly that David almost lost his footing on the rockface. "It's just a thunderstorm," he whispered as he tried to calm them, but the boys knew differently. The gods were angry with Chief Tuklit, and they were getting ready to punish his village.

After a long pause and a further hundred-foot climb, the three found themselves edging along a narrow path high above the bay, the invisible water lapping steadily against the rocks directly below them. The tireless climbers hugged the grim cool granite wall, inching their way along until, in a brilliant blue glow of sheet lightning, there appeared the triangular opening of a cave not more than ten feet ahead. The boys knelt down and crawled on all fours, one by one disappearing into the forbidding darkness of the long cavern. Once they were safely inside, a whispered argument broke out between the two native boys and quickly came to an end when one of them moved out of the shelter to act as lookout. David and the remaining village boy sat on the cold floor of the dank hollow and tried to penetrate the blackness with sleepy eyes.

In the cedar longhouses at the base of the cliffs, there were still signs of activity, particularly in the home of Tuklit. The entrance cover was pushed open, allowing the escape of the orange glow of the fire and the moving shadows of men. Inside, the frustrated chief towered over the fire pit, waiting for the return of the numerous hunting parties and the two children. He thrust his hands over the flames and ran them through his hair, the warmth of his fingers melting the crusted fish oil which matted the black strands. He plucked his spear out of the hard earth and then dug it into the ground again and began to pace back and forth, talking to himself as he went. Suddenly the rough boards were pushed away from the entrance and a single native climbed into the dimly lit chamber.

"Well?" the chief shouted at him.

"He is not in the shaman's house, Tuklit," the scout said quietly.

"Don't tell me where he is not!" Tuklit screamed. "Find him!"

"But if he is not with the shaman's people, then he has vanished. And the girl, too," the man reasoned.

"They cannot vanish. Find him. Find that boy!" the chief shot back. "Do as I say."

Just as the shaking young warrior ducked down to leave the longhouse, Klutu pushed his head through the entrance and clambered inside.

"Father, I have . . ." he began.

"Silence! You have nothing to tell me," Tuklit admonished him.

"But Father, I have . . ."

"Get out — just get out of my way."

Klutu's shoulders drooped and his head hung down as he felt the sting of his father's cruel tongue. He thought that he knew where the Spirit Child might be hiding, but now, as he picked himself up and withdrew from the longhouse in shame, he wasn't so sure he should find him and bring him to Tuklit. He moped along the pebbled beach, following the movement of the thunder as it rolled closer to the village and fear began to creep into his heart. What if some other brave found the Spirit Child and the Nootka girl? His father might adopt that warrior as his son, and Klutu would never be chief. He could not let this happen, and he thought that it was quite possible that the two were hidden in the place they would least

likely be found — the winter den of old One-Eye the bear, a
deep cavern in the cliff high above the village. Klutu would
march the prisoners before him across the village compound
and into his father's longhouse. Then all the people would see
him and praise him in front of his father. Tuklit would have to
honour him!

High on the granite cliff a young native boy huddled to one
side of the cave entrance, nervously eyeing the single path-
way, expecting at any moment a dozen of Tuklit's warriors to appear, his own brother among them. At the same
time, he wondered if old One-Eye might wish to visit his den
for an early autumn slumber. The boy drew his knees up to his
chin and shivered as a gust of wind blew into every pore of his
brown skin.

Inside the rocky shelter, David and the second of his friends
listened to the distant thunder, the English boy counting the
seconds between forked flash and booming retort. His head
was filled with plans for an escape. He would steal a canoe if
he were able or swim if he could not. Climbing the cliffs along
the water's edge would be impossible and he knew of no trail
that would take him back to the *Langley*. As he brooded, his
native partner fiddled with the reed pouch in the blackness
and pulled out a chunk of dried meat, handing it to David,
whispering as he did so. The blond boy understood the Indian
word for venison and groped about until he was able to find
the tasty morsel.

Rain began to pelt down in large drops, falling hard on the
head and shoulders of the brave watchman, who immediately
pressed his hands down on the ledge and eased himself inside.
He quickly caught a waft of the delicious venison and forgot
his duties completely, joining his friends to share in the meal.

They all chatted in low voices, using words in both Indian and English, phrases learned amid much laughter and frolic during happier days.

Without warning, a terrifying bolt of electricity shot down, lighting the granite chamber with rays as strong as the noonday sun, and there, in the glowing entrance, stood the sneering, beady-eyed Klutu, a small band of youths peering over his shoulders. Hearts sank and hopes fell, and it looked now as if all was lost.

The climb down the treacherous wall seemed much longer and more difficult than the ascent an hour before. Now here they were, being poked and pushed along down the rain-slicked trail, leather thongs bound tightly about their necks, making any slip or stumble extremely dangerous. It didn't seem to matter to their captors that they could not see where they were going, and they were given no rest until their torn feet touched the storm-soaked grass on the bluff. Immediately, David was separated from his two friends and marched by the hair to the entrance of the shaman's longhouse. Once there, Klutu slipped behind the English boy and wrapped a muscular arm around his throat, pulling him backward onto his heels. Then the bitter native youth withdrew a whalebone knife from a cord tied around his waist and held the point under the boy's chin.

"Send the Nootka slave girl out, or see the pale one die on your doorstep!" he screamed into the night.

Slowly a rough cedar panel slid back and a head appeared. A pair of eyes blinked into the darkness and then the panel closed.

"I, Klutu, son of Tuklit, warn you once more. Send her out or I kill the pale one. *Now!*"

"Oh, please," David whispered to himself. "Please hurry!"

The knife dug deeper into his skin and he felt a trickle of warm blood run down his neck.

After another terrifying moment, the door was pushed open again and the tiny figure of Nootka climbed out into the rain in halting steps. She made her way towards David and his tormentor until Klutu was able to reach out and grab her shoulder. He suddenly let David go and the boy dropped to the grass, his legs buckling like twigs. Klutu hung onto the native girl and called out to his friends.

"Return to the longhouse of my father and tell him Klutu comes with the pale one and the slave girl."

Quickly the boy was dragged up onto his feet and the two captives were herded over to the open entrance and brought before the chief. Far from the triumphant scene Klutu had imagined, Tuklit ignored his son, scarcely turning his head as he entered, so busy was he with his plans for the sacrifice and his return to power over the village.

"Prepare yourselves to meet the whale god," he said at last. "Get ready the whale canoe. Dress it with the ceremonial colours of death. When the sun rises, we will paddle to the great sea to offer the boy and the girl-slave to the killer whale."

The mournful throb of the funeral drum filled the air as the body of the shaman was carried out and laid in a small canoe lying in the shallows, its lone paddler waiting patiently. Unmoved, Tuklit's braves watched from the shadows of the houses as they walked quietly towards the whale canoe pulled high up on the beach. They were not touched by the grief of their families, for the shaman had many times put an end to their plans of raids upon unsuspecting neighbours with his talk of peace. Now they were free to let loose their fighting powers, and under Tuklit's leadership they would become respected warriors up and down the coastal waters. Soon it would be they, not the Nootka, who would be feared.

Fires were lit now that the rain had stopped, and the flames gave light to their labours. They scooped dried leaves and twigs from the unused hull and tied branches of yellow broom along its sleek toprail. The thunderbird prow began to glow in the flames as new paint sank into the porous wood, and the thick red dyes were sloshed over thirty paddles until they too glistened in the fire's reflection.

David leaned against a stubby post inside the longhouse and tried to sort out the noises coming to him out of the darkness. He wondered if the *Langley* would still be waiting for him, and then he glanced down and quickly remembered that he wasn't the only one who was in trouble. He gazed at Nootka huddled by his feet, her hair shining in the beam of silver moonlight that now found its way into the chamber. Above them both, a lone silent guard stood leaning against his spear.

The black night finally began to lose its sharpness as a grey film of light gradually fanned across the eastern sky. A very tired captive looked long at the guard, waiting for him to move, perhaps shuffle a foot or shift from one leg to the other. Then the boy's eyes widened. "He's asleep!" he thought.

He stood up very slowly, unwinding cramped limbs, and then he reached down and tapped his Nootka friend on the shoulder. "Don't worry, Nootka — I'll come back for you," he whispered.

He knew that she would not understand what he had said, but he had to try to tell her. After another quick look about, he crept noiselessly to the entrance. Once there, he took a long cool breath of fresh air before easing himself out into the open.

He listened to make sure he was not being followed, then broke into a silent run across the wet grass until his bare feet touched the cool stones of the beach. He crouched low so that he would not cast shadows as he passed the workers' fires and, when he felt secure, he bolted for the shoreline, leaping from one moonlit boulder to the next. A sleeping gull paid him no heed as it perched a few feet away from the boy's path, but David froze for a moment to make sure that the bird would not sound an alarm. He waited breathlessly, his heart pounding within him, and then he lowered a foot into the water. He waded in without a sound until he was waist-deep in the cool inlet and then silently began to swim. Strong arms reached out in a smooth breaststroke, edging him towards the grey cliffs, his head held high so that he might follow carefully the activities on the fire-lit beach.

After some hundred yards, he flipped onto his back, swimming and observing the villagers at the same time. Finding that he was not being followed, he turned over and swam on, using a powerful crawl, each long stroke giving him a renewed spirit, new hope. Behind him, the tiny orange flames of the fires dwindled to mere flickers in the grey mist.

The tireless swimmer pushed himself along with deep thrusts, more confident with each minute, and his steady kick propelled him speedily onward until he could no longer see the village in the growing daylight. At last he was alone, free, forging his way towards the far corner of the inlet where he was sure he would find the entrance to the larger body of water and the good ship anchored there. So often he had watched the canoes plying back and forth. He could not be mistaken.

David had no idea how long he had been in the water, but he knew that he had set some kind of record for himself. His heart felt as if it had been let loose from some cage, and he was sure that he was on the right course. He swam as long as he could and then climbed out onto a flat rock beneath the cliffs and hid behind a boulder while he caught his breath. He was not the only one able to snatch a few seconds of rest. A hundred yards behind him, a small seal eased its sore body into the shallows for a moment in order to lick its wound. The pup had seen David swim by the rock it was lying on, and with tremendous courage it had pulled itself slowly into the water to begin the slow, fatiguing game of chase. Gradually the cool, clean water gave the pup renewed energy and it fought on. Now it enjoyed its first respite in two long hours.

Once he was restored, David looked up and down the long, narrow waterway and waded into the warm tide to continue his watery flight. Each hundred strokes brought him closer to the end of the inlet where he knew he would find the doorway into the *Langley*'s refuge. He knew he mustn't relax his guard: he had not only the prospect of pursuit to think about, he had also to watch for incoming canoes with their catches of fish.

Suddenly, ahead of him, the first glimpse of the opening was his! He swam with new strength, moving across the water to cut down the distance, and now the outgoing tide began to sweep him up.

Twenty-Two

*T*o the west of the *Langley*, clear blue sky stretched out over clear blue ocean as far as the eye could see. To the east lay a blanket of white fog so thick that no ship, however large, would dare challenge it.

Thirty-four men stood in their best togs, caps in hand, as the shrouded body of a young sailor slipped from beneath the British ensign into deep water, forever to keep his peace. The man had not awakened from the blow he had received the night before when he was swept across the stormy deck, and now the captain read a passage from the worn Bible, committing the tar's soul to his maker. The captain closed the book and, after a moment's silence, bid the men return to their labours, for there was much to be done.

First of all, sails would have to be sewn and mounted before the ship could hoist full canvas. She could not depend upon the currents from the north to take her to the Sandwiches, no matter how powerful they might be. Already she was well off her course, and the strong tide was pushing her ever closer to the rocky coastal shores. What was worse, time was beginning to weigh heavily, everyone on board knowing well that her supplies of food and fresh water would not last forever.

Finally, the inspection of the rigging had uncovered the true damage left by the wicked storm. Two yardarms on the main had been burned beyond repair, the victims of a stray bolt of lightning. They were too weak to hold sail and, without them, the voyage across the unruly Pacific would be next to impossible. There was only one choice left for the captain, one he did not have the heart to make.

"You say the damage is that severe, bosun?" he asked for the third time.

Grimsbey answered patiently, "Aye, sir. The metal fixings be melted down as well. We'll have to see to new timber, Captain!"

"I expect that means putting a cutter to shore, sir," Perkins said as he scanned the solid wall of fog. "Certainly we have a wide choice, once we penetrate that blanket there."

The captain was silent, gazing out over the water, rubbing his chin as he summed up the situation. He regretted having to land again upon these forlorn shores. Old wounds would be opened and the pain of his loss would deepen. But he was beginning to accept that he had no choice.

"How far do you think we have drifted, sir?" Perkins broke the silence.

"Can't rightly say, Mr Perkins," the captain replied. "Can't fully trust these sextants, you know . . ."

Grimsbey tugged at the giant oak wheel, held firm and sniffed the air like a hunting hound. He nodded and grunted to himself as Captain Spencer watched him.

"Well, bosun, I expect you have it all figured out."

"Just be a guess, sir," Grimsbey said casually.

"Alright, man — speak up."

"Methinks, Captain, that just beyond that bank of fog lies the inlet itself, sir. The surf be silent over there, as you probably noticed already."

"There are some excellent trees there, and easy to reach, sir," Perkins piped up. "I hope he is right."

"I hope he is not," Captain Spencer snapped without warning. "Mr Perkins, you will take the watch. Keep an eye to the fog."

Having said his piece, the captain flung himself down the steep gangway and was quickly out of sight. Perkins glanced at Grimsbey, shrugged his shoulders and pushed his hands into his pockets. "I expect we have brought all his sad memories back to him. What a pity!"

"Deep wounds heal slow," Grimsbey said, almost to himself. "We needs the timber just the same."

"Indeed. Look, bosun, I know you have a way with him. Go below and ask his permission to cast anchor," Perkins said suddenly. "He'll listen to you."

"As you say, sir." The old man stepped down off the helm, looked back and then carried on to the aft hatch. A gentle knock on the polished oak brought no response. A second, bolder knuckle did better and the bosun was invited to enter.

"Well, Grimsbey?"

"Begging your pardon, sir, but the First Mate requests your leave to cast the anchor hereabouts."

"Why here? There are a million trees to be found along this coast! Any one of them can be fashioned into a boom. We still have enough sail on two masts to take us miles away."

"Aye, sir, but if another storm should set upon us . . ."

"It's the cross, isn't it?"

"The what, sir?"

Captain Spencer rose and walked to the chart table. "This!" he said, holding the carpenter's masterpiece towards the bearded tar.

"Well, now that you mention it, sir, we could build us a cairn for the boy. . . and hoist the cross atop it. That might put an end to the keel-hauling you be giving yourself, sir. Sort of a funeral, aye, to bury your grief, perhaps."

"I expect. . .I expect that is what the men want me to do, isn't it?"

"Only if it's what you wants for yourself, sir. It can be no other way," Grimsbey said quietly.

After a long silence, the captain strode to the great window and slowly turned around. "Very well, bosun. Tell Mr Perkins to cast anchor. We'll wait for the fog to lift and then lower a boat. Carry on!"

"Aye, sir. As you say, sir. And, uh. . ."

"Well, Grimsbey?"

"Well, thank you, sir," the bosun stammered as he pushed his cap over his head.

Twenty-Three

"The whale canoe is ready to meet the gods," a young warrior sang out.

"It is well," Tuklit answered from his raised platform. Then he turned to his son. "Klutu, bring me the children of the sacrifice. At once."

The boy leaped down off the platform and onto the path with great eagerness. He puffed out his chest as he sprinted through the fresh morning air and ducked into the opening to the longhouse. He blinked as he felt his way through the sudden darkness and then held out his hand.

"Who is there? Speak up!" the guard mumbled as he shook the sleep from his head.

"It is I, Klutu, son of Tuklit. My father sent me to bring the prisoners — at once!" Klutu answered.

"Very well. Here..." the muscular warrior nudged the small girl and commanded her to stand. Then he poked about in the darkness to find the boy. He knelt on the floor and pushed his spear to the right and left, talking to himself as he worked. He kicked out with his foot and almost lost his balance, hanging onto Klutu to pull himself upright.

"Where is the pale boy?" the teenager demanded.

"He is somewhere here...right over..." the guard mumbled.

"Light a torch, you fool!" Klutu shouted.

"Yes, a torch. Of course."

Suddenly Tuklit appeared in the doorway, the growing torchlight casting its orange glow over his hard features. "Can you not follow a simple command? A simple order?" he snarled at his first-born.

"The Spirit Child has gone, Father!"

"What do you mean, 'gone'?"

"He isn't here," the guard said meekly.

"Why you...I'll send you to the gods at once!" Tuklit screamed, raising his spear.

"Father!" Klutu shouted. "Wait — we have few warriors left. You will need him soon."

Tuklit reluctantly lowered the spear again.

"You, Klutu, summon the men to come here at once. We will search the village — every corner, every longhouse."

The early morning sunlight was beginning to flood the village, making the hunt for the boy much easier. Every corner of the compound was turned inside out, every longhouse pulled to pieces and any who might be protecting and hiding the boy were threatened with certain death. Canoes were counted and even the boys' log raft was checked. Tuklit paced back and forth across the grassy bluff above the beach, shouting and questioning his followers, both scolding them and quizzing them at the same time. He was beyond anger now, and he shook as he pounded a fist into the air.

"I can trust no one," he fumed. "Bring me the slave girl. She will be my sacrifice, and may the gods forgive me for such a foolish offering."

From the doorway of the shaman's longhouse, the peaceful villagers watched the sad procession as it moved down the pebbles to the water's edge. Young warriors, sons and older brothers of the onlookers, marched, heads high as if in a deep trance, herding the small child, who was already bound with twine. In the lead was Tuklit, clothed in his robes and head-dress, Klutu behind him, also decked in bear claw necklace and furs from shoulders to heels. All the spears were tipped with plumes, and body paint made each youth far more awesome in the eyes of the spectators. There were thirty in all, not enough to man every place in the great canoe, but a sufficient number to power the massive dugout speedily to the ocean. The villagers dared not stop Tuklit. Instead, they watched tearfully as the little girl walked to her doom. In seconds, the huge log vessel was rolled down the beach and lifted up as she was floated on the tide.

Three miles away an exhausted boy pushed through the water, his arms two pieces of stone, his legs numb and cold. Each long breath was a chore, each turn of the head a painful task. David finally edged towards the shore and pressed white, wrinkled fingers onto hot granite. He hung on for a long while, able to do nothing more until his tired muscles had time to find even a little strength. He gazed up at the high cliffs, searching for a path or at least some level piece of land upon which he might walk, if only for a few yards. Nowhere could he find an opening, not so much as a crack in the hundred-foot-high walls. Now he understood why only canoes were used to carry the tribesmen back and forth, and why there were no guards posted around the village. No enemy could hike into the head of the inlet to attack, and David was certain now that swimming was his only means of escape.

He slowly dragged his water-logged body high onto the

stone ledge and lay down on his stomach, his blurred vision now coming into focus. He felt the warmth from the sun-heated stone soak into his body and soon his skin tingled as feeling returned, limb by limb. He shut his eyes but was afraid to fall asleep lest he be captured. Instead, he thought about his mother, alone in England, and about what she would think if she knew where he was right now. He thought about the *Langley* and wondered fearfully if he would arrive at the anchorage to find her gone. He thought about his father, about Grimsbey and Walters, and his seal pup. Why hadn't the pup come when he called it?

He rolled onto his back and flicked a piece of shell from his belly. Hoisting himself up on his elbows, he glanced down at his brown skin, deeply tanned from head to toes, darker than it had ever been. How would his father know who he was, he thought, and a smile spread across his face. He noticed muscles where there were none before. Why, he was strong enough to take on Walters, or maybe Link.

An eagle floated on the breeze high above his head, soaring silently towards the mouth of the inlet. The boy followed the flight of this king of birds, then thought about his own mission. The sun was high and it was time to continue his watery journey. Climbing to his feet, he stretched and scanned the inlet for any sign of a canoe. For the moment at least, he was free. The villagers had seemed so angry with each other that he didn't think they would care about him at all. Then he thought about Nootka and how she must have felt when she realized he had gone. He must hurry!

He waded into the silky warm water and dove down. Soon he was speeding along the cliffs with new-found strength, knowing that after another mile, maybe less, he would be safe in the wide sound that led to the ocean. Eighty or ninety yards behind him, a small animal struggled to stay afloat, swimming short sprints and then turning on its back to rest. Its round glassy eyes were set on the light splash from the young boy's feet ahead of it. The sight spurred it on.

The mighty canoe lumbered through the inlet, closing swiftly on the narrow passage opening into the sound. Sweating warriors leaned into their work, never paddling hard enough to suit their master, who sat restfully on the bowsprit beside his lazy son.

"Father, what is that?" Klutu asked suddenly.

"I did not ask you to speak. I am in prayer," the chief snapped.

After a few seconds of silence, the boy tried again. "But Father — see it? Over there," he exclaimed as he pointed to a disturbance on the water in the narrow channel.

"Silence, I said!" Tuklit wiped his knife blade on his fat stomach, then twisted around. "Well, speak up. What do you see?"

"It's a swimmer! See him?"

Tuklit squinted into the reflection on the water and then stood up. "Ahhh! Warriors, swing the canoe towards the side of the channel. More power, but be quiet."

Silently, the eight-foot vessel shortened the distance and the natives quickly recognized the blond hair flowing on top of the water as the boy moved steadily ahead. The chief ordered the men to hold their paddles out of the water, allowing the massive dugout to creep noiselessly up beside the unsuspecting fugitive. The natives gleefully watched the boy as he swam below them, turning his head towards the shore each time he breathed, unaware of his certain recapture. After some three minutes, the young swimmer rolled onto his back to rest and gasped as he looked up at thirty red- and black-streaked faces leering down at him.

Instead of yanking the terrified boy out of the water, the chief elected to let him keep swimming. The warriors paddled slowly along as the boy continued his journey, his arms and legs drained of their energy. He glanced up at them, then carried on for a few more yards. Finally, he thrashed the water with his fist and moved four feet over to the log hull, reached up to be roughly hoisted into the massive vessel and passed along to the stern like a sack of potatoes. He was quickly trussed and dropped onto the burned decking beside a heavy net which seemed to be wrapped around a foot, a leg. . . It was Nootka, bundled up in a round ball, her wrists tightly bound. She peeked through the vine prison at her friend and then shut her eyes.

As the massive canoe eased ahead once more, its cargo now complete, a tiny head popped up through the surface of the water behind it, and a tired, fat little body gathered new energy, slowly swimming below the barren cliffs.

Twenty-Four

"*P*repare to haul the timber aboard, Mr Wiggins," the captain called out from his perch amidships. "Sailor, secure the painter there."

The longboat hovered close to the *Langley*'s hull, six oars held vertically before being shipped. Behind the cutter floated three heavy logs, all forty feet in length, still covered in thick brown bark, sap running freely from their stumps. As the pulleys were being rigged and a boom pushed out over the water, Captain Spencer looked about for the carpenter. "Glennesk — you there!"

"Aye, sir?"

"Put the men to stripping the bark at once. It'll take them a good hour. That should give you enough time to accompany the men ashore."

"Ashore, sir?" Perkins said as he walked over to the captain. "I thought three logs would do, sir."

"True, Mr Perkins, but have you forgotten? The men

would have Glennesk's cross planted on the beach somewhere."

"Why, yes. Yes, of course, sir."

"Then, if you don't mind, Perkins, you might go down to
my quarters and fetch the piece. It lies on the chart table."

Grimsbey was listening with rapt attention, delighted with
his captain's change of heart. "Excuse me, sir, but I expects you
will take the men in, sir?"

"I thought you would do that, bosun." Captain Spencer
turned to him as he spoke.

"Aye, but it wouldn't be the same, sir. I mean, well, being
your son and all. . ." the old sailor answered carefully.

"Ah, yes. You're right, my man. If you will select six
worthies, we will ship out at once. Hurry up, Mr Perkins.
Come along, Glennesk!"

"Very good, sir," the carpenter grinned as he clambered
over the rail. He shinnied down the heavy line and dropped
himself into the boat, Grimsbey close behind him. The captain
was next, and when he was settled the wooden cross was
lowered down until he could reach out and take it safely onto
his lap. With all hands aboard, Grimsbey placed the palm of
his hand against the *Langley*'s black hull and with a mighty
push set the cutter free of her.

"Lay to the oars, men," the captain ordered in a quiet voice.

The *Langley* immediately weighed anchor and began to
tack slowly southward with as little sail as possible. She would
come north again and follow this zigzag pattern so that she
might keep a weather eye on the small boat and her nine-man
crew. Her officers and men lined the railing at the port side,
all wishing that they too might have a part in this final act
of farewell.

Over and down the cutter skidded, into deep watery

troughs and then onto the tops of jagged crests, the spray flying off the oars. Suddenly the little craft was picked up on the incoming tide roaring through the narrow channel, and she glided smoothly along until she was safe on the calm waters of the familiar inlet.

Once swallowed up in the serene beauty of the place, the crew quickly set to the oars, knifing swiftly towards a small white sandy beach. The tillerman, Peters, sat beside Captain Spencer, his red hair flying in the light breeze. He scanned the shallows for a safe landing spot and then looked about. Something caught his eye.

"Captain, sir?" he said quietly.

"Aye, m'lad?"

"What do you make of that, sir?"

"What do you see? Ah, yes — yes indeed!" the captain answered as he automatically pulled his glass from his jacket. "Our Indian friends . . . mmmm. Grimsbey? Look to starboard there."

"Just a moment, sir. Alright. My goodness, sir! That is a mighty log canoe if ever I laid eyes on one, sir!" the bosun gasped.

"Looks quite ordinary to me, Grimsbey," Captain Spencer replied.

"Maybe at first glance, if you'll pardon me, sir, but have you counted the troops they have aboard? I gets thirty if I gets one, sir."

"Hah! You are quite right. And look there — they are coming about. I think they are heading right for us!"

The men watched the rapidly advancing craft in silence, each one awaiting word from the captain. The colourful design on the canoe's prow was clearly visible now, and the voices of the paddlers spilled out over the water. They were

shouting, and some of them waved long spears. Finally
Captain Spencer took his eyes off them.

"Doesn't look as if they're bearing gifts," he said calmly.
"Peters, tiller full starboard. I think we'd best seek the shelter
of the ship for the moment."

Grimsbey eyed the ever-advancing canoe. "We have the
tide against us, Captain. It'll take some row."

"Then we will give it 'some row' as you say, Grimsbey.
All right, men. Backs to it!"

The heavily armed canoe raced onward through the inlet
towards the little cutter, the natives tasting the battle that
Tuklit had promised them.

"*Hiiieeeee!*" Klutu screamed as he stood on the high prow.

"*Hiiieeeee!*" the paddlers screamed after him.

For the moment they had forgotten their sacrifices to the
whale gods, who huddled nervously on the dank wood at the
stern. David lay perfectly still, his fingers working the dry
vines, strand by brittle strand. He watched Nootka as she bit
into the tight cord that bound her small wrists, and wondered
how long it would be before they passed the *Langley* at anchor. He ached to climb up high enough to look out on the
water, but every time he raised himself a little, the last paddler
glanced down, so he dared not take any more chances.

Nootka managed to break through the last of her bonds just
as David pulled his hand out of a rough cedar loop. Together
they worked at the netting, the boy checking behind him to
make sure they were not being observed. Finally, the covering
loosened and both boy and girl were able to move almost freely. Above them, the activity increased until the canoe fairly
throbbed with the commotion, heaving from side to side with
the rhythm of the paddlers as they dipped into the water.

Tuklit stood, feet astride, and wet his lips as he drank in the pleasure of pending slaughter. He shook a fist at the desperate white cutter as she drew closer. His eyes gleamed as he imagined himself dressed in the strangers' clothing, a broad black hat atop his head-dress! He swung around and screamed an order above the din. Instantly, ten of the young men lay down their paddles and took up tufted spears, standing as they did so.

"Ready, my warriors, for the attack!" he bellowed in a terrible howl that resounded across the water.

The nine Englishmen were stirred by this last outburst and redoubled their efforts. The cutter's bow ripped through the still green water, six oarsmen working in perfect time, all leaning back as one man, pulling with all their might. The captain and Peters clung to the tiller, holding her steady, while Grimsbey called time, his booming voice solid and unshaking.

Behind them the monstrous canoe closed the distance, now no more than thirty yards away, and the Englishmen could see the natives standing at the ready, their spears held at their sides. Sweat ran down the sides of the exhausted tars. One man in the back slumped down in defeat and Captain Spencer tore off his jacket, shoved the fellow aside and took his oar. "Come on, chaps, put your backs into it!" he cried.

"She be coming on us, Captain," Grimsbey warned.

"You have a musket up there?"

"Aye aye, sir."

"Very well — send a shot over their heads!"

Grimsbey fussed with the wad of powder, half-stood on the tilting prow and dug a foot solidly into the gunnel. He let off a mighty blast which was immediately doubled by a deafening echo. When the smoke cleared, Indians could be seen swimming away from the speeding canoe. Their brothers sat in stunned silence, allowing their massive dugout to come to a slow drift. Tuklit lay flat on his stomach for a moment until he could gather his wits about him. Then he climbed to his feet, screaming oaths over the heads of the fleeing swimmers and ordering the remaining paddlers back to their task.

In the rear of the native craft, David had recognized the noise of the gun instantly and was now on his feet, shouting at the top of his lungs. But the cutter was speedily moving away from the weakened Indian vessel, and Grimsbey's rhythmic exhortations drowned out the boy's calls. Nootka lay at his feet, huddling and cringing in fear, her ears still filled with the thunderous message from the gods. David watched with despair as the British boat moved farther and farther away.

Tuklit ordered spears into the air and watched them fall short, knifing the water harmlessly, feet away from the white hull. Next he looked down at his son and cried out, "You, boy! Go down there and kill the slave boy — we will make the sacrifice now! Go, I say!"

Out on the ocean, the *Langley* eased past the mouth of the inlet on her second run northward. While Perkins casually worked the sextant, Wiggins stood at the rail, the ship's glass to his eye. He found it difficult to focus on the inlet while the *Langley* rolled under his feet, but when he finally succeeded, he was puzzled by what he saw. It looked for all the world like some sort of attack from a native barge. He waited for a moment and then took a second try at the glass.

"I say, Perkins?" he said finally.

"Wait a bit," Perkins muttered. "I'm getting a fix here..."

"But you should see this. I don't quite know what to make of it."

"Here — let me see," the First Officer grumbled as he took the glass. "I say!"

"You agree?" Wiggins crowed happily.

"Indeed I do, old man." Then Perkins ran to the forward

rail. "Ahoy, chaps! Loosen all sail. Dandry, Wilkes — take your men to the starboard cannon. Light up and wait for orders. Step to it!"

"We can blow those blighters right out of the water, what?" Wiggins said as he rubbed his hands together.

"Without hitting the cutter? I don't think so. Best we send a shot over their heads. Stand ready to fire!"

Twenty-Five

*I*nside the inlet, the dugout was once again closing the distance between itself and the slowing English cutter, the remaining fifteen young men bending sinewy arms to the paddles, jaws set firm, eyes fixed on the white longboat. Klutu climbed between them, over one cross-timber and then another. He grasped his knife in his clenched fist and squinted as he focused on the back of the pale boy, who was hurriedly working loose the thick vine that secured Nootka to a massive granite boulder. As Klutu reached the last paddler, Nootka glanced up and shrieked. David turned about to see the Indian youth flying through the air towards him, his knife held high. The young prisoner dropped onto his back and drew his knees to his chest, then thrust his legs outward like two coiled springs and caught the crazed Klutu in the stomach with both feet, sending the surprised attacker skyrocketing over the side of the canoe into the water.

Tuklit gasped as he watched his son hurtling through the air, then snatched a spear from the nearest warrior, his face distorted by rage. He lumbered down the centre of the teetering craft, stepping on arms and knees as he went, until he was within feet of David. The dazed chief poised himself and raised the ugly, stone-tipped spear, but at that moment a thunderous boom reverberated across the water.

The huge native was frozen to the spot. His wide, awe-stricken eyes were filled with the sight of a giant fir tree splitting into two pieces as it fell into the water a few yards from his beleaguered dugout. His remaining warriors, now completely shattered, leaped out of their demon canoe and swam away in a dozen different directions. David grasped Nootka's hand, pulling her onto her feet in one swift motion.

"We have to jump — jump, Nootka. Come on!" he pleaded to the girl, but she could not bring herself to move a muscle. The boy sighed and then glanced behind him to see Tuklit crawling towards them on his hands and knees. David wrapped his arm around her shoulder and leaped out, pulling her with him. They struck the water well clear of the drifting canoe and both began to swim in the direction of the white longboat.

In the cutter, six exhausted men, the captain among them, sat with their heads on their knees, too breathless to speak. Grimsbey surveyed the thrashing arms and legs in the water, the floating branches of the great fir and the drifting canoe a hundred yards away. He shook his head in disbelief. Dozens of heads bobbed on the waves, slowly making way to the cliffs beyond, all of them churning along — except, that is, for one or two swimmers near the abandoned canoe. The old bosun scratched his head, thankful indeed that all hands were spared.

"*Stop!*" David screamed over the shouts of the fleeing warriors. "Help us, please help us!"

The English boy waved desperately as he swam, keeping

Nootka beside him. He would not believe that after all that had happened to him, the *Langley* would leave him here now. They couldn't leave him — they couldn't!

He glanced behind him and saw, not more than ten feet away, Klutu, swimming with powerful strokes, his bone-handled knife clenched between his teeth. The Indian boy lunged blindly ahead, and as he closed in, he raised his arm for the final blow. Just as he did so, he cried out in pain and curled up into a ball, his head disappearing beneath the surface. David thrashed ahead, but again the native boy surfaced and swam towards him, this time without the wicked blade. He was now only inches from David and Nootka, his steely eyes never leaving them. He reached out for David's throat, but again he cringed, rolled over and ducked under, grasping his stomach as he did so. David pulled away from him, then stopped short: a round, shiny grey head had bobbed up in front of his face and touched its nose to his cheek. After the first shock of recognition, David began to piece things together. It must have been the seal pup that had nipped Klutu, forcing him to give up his deadly pursuit! Now the little animal circled around and around the two tiring swimmers, happy to be close to its master again. Together, the three swam on, the boy hoping and praying for one last reprieve.

The cutter's crew rowed easily now, having no need to rush back to the ship. They would wait until the natives had made up their minds to leave the inlet to the longboat, and then they would select a likely spot to place the cross. Grimsbey kept watch, scanning the bay for signs of any new danger.

"Captain, sir?" he said after a long silence.

"What is it, bosun?"

"Captain, what do you make of that over there?" Grimsbey asked as he pointed a finger.

The captain followed his gaze and squinted in silence for

a moment. Then, suddenly, he was on his feet, his glass raised.

"Men! Stand to — wake up! Full oars. Peters, swing her about full."

"What do you see, sir?" Peters asked as he leaned on the tiller.

"Peters, my good chap, I see a native boy out there with a head of blond hair — that's what I see!" the captain roared as he handed over the glass. "Here, see for yourself."

"I'll be a goner, man — you're ruddy well right!" Peters exclaimed before he quickly recovered himself with, "I mean, sir, I beg your pardon, sir."

"You'll have my pardon, my good chap, if you steer us a straight course," Captain Spencer replied with a grin.

"Aye, sir. That I will do!"

Grimsbey leaned over towards Glennesk, who was pulling the starboard bow oar. "Methinks you'll have to find another use for your cross, there."

"Aye, bosun, and thank goodness for that!"

After a few anxious seconds, the cutter eased to a standstill beside the haggard, worn swimmers, and strong arms pulled them gently to safety. David was numb, scarcely able to register what was happening as he was passed along from man to man towards the stern. There his father swept him into his arms and pressed him to his chest. At the same time, Grimsbey lifted Nootka onto his own lap and pulled his jacket over her shivering shoulders.

"Davie. . .Davie. . .Davie. . ." the captain repeated over and over. His tears mixed with the salt water running down the boy's cheeks. "My son, my own dear son!"

David drew a long breath and looked up at his father. "I'm sorry about these leggings, sir," he said quietly as he fingered the ragged strings at his waist.

At this the entire crew, including the captain, burst into

laughter, releasing weeks of tension and despair. David could not believe his ears and gazed up into his father's grinning face to make sure it truly was the captain's.

Once the laughter had subsided, Captain Spencer asked, "Davie, who have we there with Grimsbey?"

"She's my friend, sir. I call her Nootka because I think she belongs to the Nootka people up north," David answered. "She helped me a lot, especially when I first arrived at the village — oh, you don't even know about that yet! We can take her home, can't we Father?"

"Home to England?" Captain Spencer asked gently.

"No, I mean to Nootka Sound. We can, can't we?"

"Methinks, if you'll pardon me, sir, we've already done our tour of Nootka Sound. We be on our way home to England, aye," Grimsbey broke in with a wink.

"Ah, but you forget, bosun, I have yet to pay my respects to Chief Maquinna," the captain answered as seriously as he could. "Very well, Davie, my lad, Nootka Sound it shall be!"

David sighed with relief and then, leaning against the captain's chest, he shut his eyes. Looking down at him, his father wondered what he must have endured. He looked ten pounds heavier, with broad shoulders and powerful limbs. But there would be plenty of time to hear the whole story later — and time also for the captain to make up for his stern coldness in the past.

"Look, Davie — there's your seal pup!"

David twisted about to see the seal swimming alongside the cutter. He reached over and let his hand skim along the surface, and a wet nose nuzzled his fingers, then fell away, the little animal slowly putting distance between itself and the longboat.

The boy sat up again. "It saved my life, Father. Nootka's too."

"And now it's returning to its inlet. See it there?" Captain Spencer leaned back to allow the boy a better view of the silver-grey head.

David sank back against his father's strong shoulder, his eyes following the tiny dot on the surface of the calm inlet until it slipped out of sight.

"Good-bye, little seal . . . good-bye."

Epilogue

*H*igh up on the wide beach opposite the *Langley*, three ragged slaves trundled along over a series of boulders, two of them hidden beneath massive loads of driftwood. The third followed, picking up the odd piece that had fallen from the stooped shoulders of the bearers ahead. All of them paused long enough to gaze out at the shiny white cutter as it drew up alongside the sailing ship. One of the rough-robed onlookers took a swipe at his nose with his hand to shoo away a pesky sand flea.

"Huh!" he snorted. "Would you look at that now?"

"Aye, Link," Havlock answered sullenly. "I sees it."

"Come on, you two, or we'll catch a drubbing from the master. He's just around the corner there!" Walters warned them.

"Sure, and how about your lifting a load or two yourself?" Havlock growled at him.

"Mind your mouth, mate. Somebody here has to do the thinking," Walters answered.

"Aye, that's right, but for me, I says we hail the ship and give ourselves up."

Walters sat down on a log. "That'd be first rate, that would. You, me and Havlock here strung up to the yardarm for mutiny!"

"Maybe better'n being slaves for the rest of our days, eh?" Link grumbled.

"Ahh, you just stick with me," Walters assured him. "Soon we'll find ourselves a Spaniard brig and make way to home. Then we gets even with Spencer and that brat of his. Who knows? Someday we may take the gold out of —"

Just then a sharp pebble struck Walters on the back of the neck. He slapped a hand over the spot and spat on a log. "Come on, you lazy louts — get them sticks moving there!"